MAX

The James Patterson Pageturners

The Maximum Ride Novels

The Angel Experiment

School's Out—Forever

Saving the World and Other Extreme Sports

The Final Warning

MAX

The Daniel X Novels

The Dangerous Days of Daniel X
(with Michael Ledwidge)

Daniel X: Watch the Skies (with Ned Rust)

Also by James Patterson

When the Wind Blows

The Lake House

For previews of upcoming books by James Patterson and more information about the author, visit www.jamespatterson.com.

MAX

A MAXIMUM RIDE NOVEL

James Patterson

LITTLE, BROWN AND COMPANY
NEW YORK BOSTON LONDON

Little, Brown and Company
Hachette Book Group
237 Park Avenue, New York, NY 10017
Visit our Web site at www.HachetteBookGroup.com

First Edition: March 2009

Little, Brown and Company is a division of Hachette Book Group, Inc. The Little, Brown name and logo are trademarks of Hachette Book Group, Inc.

Library of Congress Cataloging-in-Publication Data
Patterson, James.
MAX : a Maximum Ride novel / James Patterson. — 1st ed.
p. cm.
Summary: When millions of fish start dying off the coast of Hawaii and something is destroying hundreds of ships, the government enlists the flock — a band of genetically modified children who can fly — to help get to the bottom of the mystery before it is too late.
ISBN 978-0-316-00289-9
[1. Marine animals — Fiction. 2. Genetic engineering — Fiction. 3. Adventure and adventurers — Fiction. 4. Hawaii — Fiction. 5. Science fiction.] I. Title.
PZ7.P27653Mas 2009
[Fic] — dc22

2008042316

10 9 8 7 6 5 4 3 2 1

RRD-IN

Printed in the United States of America

To Joshua Chamberlain Perry

Many thanks to Gabrielle Charbonnet,
my conspirator, who flies high and cracks wise.
And to Mary Jordan, for brave assistance
and research at every twist and turn.

To the reader

THE IDEA FOR the Maximum Ride series comes from earlier books of mine called *When the Wind Blows* and *The Lake House*, which also feature a character named Max who escapes from a quite despicable School. Most of the similarities end there. Max and the other kids in the Maximum Ride books are not the same Max and kids featured in those two books. Nor do Frannie and Kit play any part in the series. I hope you enjoy the ride anyway.

Prologue

THE MADNESS NEVER STOPS

Near Los Angeles Basin, California

THERE.

Devin raised his right arm and focused directly over his wrist. It took less than a millisecond to calculate the trajectory—he didn't have a built-in computer, but his 220 IQ served him well.

He slowly breathed in and out, getting ready to squeeze the trigger between breaths, between heartbeats. His sensitive nose wrinkled as the ever-present smog that hovered over the Los Angeles Basin filled his lungs. He hated to think what the pollutants were doing to his brain cells but accepted that some things were necessary evils.

There.

His light eyes expertly tracked the objects flying overhead: one, two, three, four, five, six. Seven? There was a small seventh object, unexpected but quickly determined to be unimportant. Actually, all of them were unimportant. All but one. The one in front.

He knew they had raptor vision. He merely had

extraordinary eyesight. It was good enough. All the same, the crosshairs in the gun sight attached to his wrist made missing an impossibility. He never missed.

That's why they saved him for extraspecial missions like this one.

Many, many others had already failed at this task. Devin felt utter disdain for them. To kill one bird kid—how hard could it be? They were flesh and blood, ridiculously fragile. It wasn't like bullets bounced off them.

Once more Devin raised his arm and observed his prey, catching her neatly in the crosshairs, as if they could pin her to the sky. The flock flew, perfectly spaced, in a large arc overhead, the one called Maximum in front, flanked by the two large males. Then a smaller female. Then a smaller male, and the smallest female after him.

A little black object, not bird kid shaped, struggled to keep up. Devin couldn't identify it—it hadn't been in his dossier. The closest thing he could imagine was if someone grafted wings onto a small dog or something, as unlikely as that was.

But Max was the only one he was concerned with. It was Max he was supposed to kill, Max whom he kept catching in his sights.

Devin sighed and lowered his arm. This was almost too easy. It wasn't sporting. He loved the chase, the hunt, the split-second intersection of luck and skill that allowed him to exercise his perfection, his inability to miss.

He looked down at what used to be his right hand. One could get used to having no right hand. It was surprisingly easy. And it was so superior to have this lovely weapon instead.

It wasn't as crude as simply having a Glock 18 grafted to the stump of an amputated limb. It was so much more elegant than that, so much more a miracle of design and ingenuity. This weapon was a part of him physically, responsive to his slightest thought, triggered by almost imperceptible nerve firings in the interface between his arm and the weapon.

He was a living work of art. Unlike the bird kids flying in traceable patterns overhead.

Devin had seen the posters, the advertisements. Those naive, do-gooder idiots at the Coalition to Stop the Madness had organized this whole thing, this air show, this demonstration of supposedly "evolved" humans.

Wrong. The bird kids were ill-conceived accidents. He, Devin, was truly an evolved human.

The CSM zealots were wasting their time—and everyone else's. Using the bird kids to promote their own agenda was a typically selfish, shortsighted thing to do. Manipulating and taking advantage of lesser creatures in order to "save" even lesser creatures? It was a joke.

A joke that could not be perpetrated without this flock of examples. And the flock could not survive without its leader.

Once again Devin raised his arm and closed his left eye to focus through the gun sight on his wrist. He angled the Glock a millimeter to the left and smoothly tracked his target as she arced across the sky.

One breath in, one breath out. One heartbeat, two heartbeats, and here we go...

Part One

FREAKS AND M-GEEKS

1

"AND A-ONE, and a-two—" Nudge said, leaning into a perfect forty-five-degree angle. Her tawny russet wings glowed warmly in the afternoon sunlight.

Behind her, the Gasman made squealing-brakes sounds as he dropped his feet down and slowed drastically. "Hey! Watch gravity in action!" he yelled, folding his wings back to create an unaerodynamic eight-year-old, his blond hair blown straight up by the wind.

I rolled my eyes. "Gazzy, stick to the choreography!" He was sinking fast, and I had to bellow to make sure he heard me. "This is a paying job! Don't blow it!" Okay, they were paying us mostly in doughnuts, but let's not quibble.

Even from this high up, I could hear the exclamations of

surprise, the indrawn gasps that told me our captive audience below had noticed one of us dropping like a rock.

I'd give him five seconds, and then I'd swoop down after him. One . . . two . . .

I wasn't sure about this whole air-show thing to begin with, but how could I refuse my own mom? After our last "working vacation" in Ant-freaking-arctica, my mom and a bunch of scientists had created an organization called the Coalition to Stop the Madness, or CSM. Basically, they were trying to tell the whole world about the dangers of pollution, greenhouse gases, dependence on foreign oil—you get the picture.

Already, more than a thousand scientists, teachers, senators, and regular people had joined the CSM. One of the teacher-members had come up with the traveling air-show idea to really get the message out. I mean, Blue Angels, Schmue Angels, but *flying mutant bird kids?* Come on! Who's gonna pass that up?

So here we were, flying perfect formations, doing tricks, air dancing, la la la, the six of us and Total, whose wings by now had pretty much finished developing. He could fly, at least, but he wasn't exactly Baryshnikov. If Baryshnikov had been a small, black, Scottie dog with wings, that is.

By the time I'd counted to four, the Gasman had ended his free fall and was soaring upward again, happiness on his relatively clean face.

Hanging out with the CSM folks had some benefits, chiefly food and decent places to sleep. And, of course, seeing my mom, which I'd never be able to get enough of, after living the first fourteen years of my life not even knowing she existed. (I explained all this in earlier books, if you want to go get caught up.)

"Yo," said Fang, hovering next to me.

My heart gave a little kick as I saw how the sun glinted off his deeply black feathers. Which matched his eyes. And his hair. "You enjoying being a spokesfreak?" I asked him casually, looking away.

One side of his mouth moved: the Fang version of unbridled chortling.

He shrugged. "It's a job."

"Yep. So long as they don't worry about pesky child labor laws," I agreed. We're an odd little band, my fellow flock members and I. Fang, Iggy, and I are all fourteen, give or take. So officially, technically, legally, we're minors. But we've been living on our own for years, and regular child protection laws just don't seem to apply to us. Come to think of it, many regular grown-up laws don't seem to apply to us either.

Nudge is eleven, roughly. The Gasman is eightish. Angel is somewhere in the six range. I don't know how old Total is, and frankly, what with the calculations of dog years into human years, I don't care.

Suddenly, out of nowhere, Angel dropped down onto me with all her forty-one pounds of feathery fun.

"Oof! What are you doing, goofball?" I exclaimed, dipping about a foot. Then I heard it: the high-pitched, all-too-familiar whine of a bullet streaking past my ear, close enough to knock some of my hair aside.

In the next second, Total yelped piercingly, spinning in midair, his small black wings flapping frantically. Angel's quick instincts had saved my life. But Total had taken the hit.

2

IN THE BLINK OF AN EYE, I rolled a full 360, spinning in the air, swooping to catch Total and also performing evasive maneuvers that, sadly, I've had way too much practice doing.

"Scatter!" I shouted. "Get out of firing range!"

We all peeled away, our wings moving fast and powerfully, gaining altitude like rockets. I heard applause floating up to me—they thought this was part of the act. Then, I looked down at the limp black dog in my arms.

"Total!" I said, holding his chunky little body. "Total!"

He blinked and moaned. "I'm hit, Max. They got me. I guess I'm gonna live fast, die young, and leave a beautiful corpse, huh?"

Okay. In my experience, if you're really hit or seriously

hurt, you don't say much. Maybe a few bad words. Maybe grunting sounds. You don't manage pithy quotes.

Quickly I shifted him this way and that, scanning for wounds. He had both ears, and his face was fine. I patted along his wings, which still looked too short to keep him aloft. Bright red blood stained my sleeve, but so far he seemed to be in one unperforated piece.

"Tell Akila," Total gasped, eyelids fluttering, "tell her she's always been the only one." Akila is the Alaskan Malamute Total had fallen for back on the *Wendy K.*, the boat where we lived with a bunch of scientists on our way to Antarctica.

"Shh," I said. "I'm still looking for holes."

"I don't have many regrets," Total rambled weakly. "True, I thought about a career in the theater, once our adventures waned. I know it's just a crazy dream, but I always hoped for just one chance to play the Dane before I died."

"Play the huh?" I said absently, feeling his ribs. Nothing broken. "Is that a game?"

Total moaned and closed his eyes.

Then I found it: the source of the blood, the place where he'd been shot.

"Total?" I said, and got a slight whimper. "You have a boo-boo on your tail."

"What?" He opened his eyes and curled to peer at his short tail. He wagged it experimentally, outrage appearing on his face as he realized a tiny chunk of flesh was missing near the tip. "I'm hit! I'm bleeding! Those scoundrels will pay for this!"

"I think a Band-Aid is probably all you need." I struggled to keep a straight face.

Fang swerved closer to me, big and supremely graceful, like a black panther with wings.

Oh, God. I'm so stupid. Forget I just said that.

"How's he doing?" Fang asked, nodding at Total.

"He needs a Band-Aid," I said. A look passed between me and Fang, full of suppressed humor, relief, understanding, *love*—

Forget I said that too. I don't know what's wrong with me.

"Got your sniper," Fang went on, pointing downward.

I shifted into battle mode. "One sniper or a whole flotilla of baddies?"

"Only see the one."

I raised an eyebrow. "So, what, we're not worth a whole flotilla anymore?" I looked down at Total. "Wings out, spud. You gotta fly on your own."

Total gathered himself with dignity, extended his wings, and jumped awkwardly out of my arms. He flapped frantically, then with more confidence, and rose to keep up with us.

"What's up?" Iggy had coasted on an updraft for a while, but now he and the others were forming a bird-kid sandwich around me.

"Total's okay," I reported. "One sniper below. Now we gotta go take him out."

Angel's pure-white wing brushed against me. She gave me a sweet smile that melted my heart, and I tried to remember that this kid had many layers, not all of them made of gumdrops and roses.

"Thanks, lamby," I said, and she grinned.

"I felt something bad about to happen," she explained. "Can we go get that guy now?"

"Let's do it," I said, and we angled ourselves downward. Among the many genetic enhancements we sport, the mad scientists who created us had thoughtfully included raptor vision. I raked the land below, almost a mile down, and traced the area where Fang pointed.

I saw him: a lone guy in the window of a building close to the air base. He was tracking us, and we began our evasive actions, dropping suddenly, swerving, angling different ways, trying to be as unpredictable as possible. We're fairly good at being unpredictable.

"Mass zoom?" Fang asked, and I nodded.

"Ig, mass zoom, angle down about thirty-five degrees. Then aim for six o'clock," I instructed. And why was I only giving Iggy instructions? Because Iggy's the only blind one, that's why.

We were moving fast, really fast, dropping at a trajectory that would smash us into the sniper's window in about eight seconds. We'd practiced racing feet-first through open windows a thousand times, one right after the other, *bam bam bam*. So this was more of a fun challenge than a scary, death-defying act of desperation.

The two things often look very similar in our world.

Seven, six, five, I counted silently.

When I got to *four,* the window exploded outward, knocking me head over heels.

3

THREE DAYS LATER...

Here, in no particular order, is a massively incomplete list of things that make me twitchy:

1) Being indoors, almost anywhere
2) Places with no easy exits
3) People who promise me tons of "benefits" and assume that I don't see right through the crapola to the stark truth that actually they want me to do a bunch of stuff for them
4) Being dressed up

So it won't take a lot of imagination on your part to guess how I reacted to our appointment at a Hollywood talent agency.

"Come in, guys," said the most gorgeous woman I've ever seen. She flashed glowing white teeth and tossed back her perfect, auburn hair as she ushered us through the heavy wooden door. "I'm Sharon. Welcome!"

I could see her trying to avoid looking at our various bruises, scrapes, and cuts. Well, if you're six feet away from a building when it *explodes* at you, you're gonna get a little banged up. Fact of life.

We were in a big office building in Hollywood. If you've been keeping up with our nutty, action-packed shenanigans, you'll remember how many *incredibly bad* experiences we've had inside office buildings. They're pretty much my least favorite place to be, right after dungeons and hospitals, but before dog crates and science labs. Call me quirky.

A member of the CSM had a friend who had a friend who had a cousin who was married to someone who knew someone at this huge, important Hollywood talent agency and volunteered us for an interview, without asking us. The CSM thought we spokesbirds were doing a bang-up job of getting their message out. Emphasis on *bang*, given the suicide sniper. But more on that later.

"Come in! Come in!" A short, balding guy in a flashy suit waved us in, big smile in place. I ratcheted up my DEFCON level to orange. "I'm Steve Blackman."

There were four of them altogether, three guys and Sharon with the great hair. She blinked when Total trotted in after us, a small white bandage still covering the tip of his tail. He'd gotten more mileage out of that weensy flesh wound than I've gotten out of broken ribs.

"Good God," I heard Total mutter as he looked at the woman. "She can't be real."

"Max!" said Steve, holding out his hand. "May I call you Max?"

"No." I frowned and looked at his hand until he pulled it back.

The other two guys introduced themselves, and we just stood there, unsmiling. Actually, Nudge smiled a little. She loves stuff like this. She'd even worn a skirt. Angel was wearing a pink tutu over her jeans. My clothes were at least clean and not blood-spattered, which is about as good as it ever gets with me.

"Well!" said Steve, rubbing his hands together. "Let's sit down and get to know each other, huh? Can we get you something to drink? You kids hungry?"

"We're always hungry," said the Gasman seriously.

Steve looked taken aback. "Ah, yes, of course! Growing kids!" He was trying hard not to look at our wings, with limited success. He reached over and tapped a button on his desk, which was so big you could practically land a chopper on it. "Jeff? How about some drinks and snacks in here? Thanks."

"Please, sit down," Sharon said, with another hair toss. I made a mental note to practice doing that in a mirror the next time I saw one. It seemed a useful skill, right up there with roundhouse kicks.

We sat, making sure no one was in back of us or could sneak up on us. I was wound so tight I was about to break out in hives.

A young guy in a purple-striped shirt came in with a tray of sodas, glasses of ice, and little nibbly things on several plates. "They're tapas," he explained. "This one's calamari, and this one's—"

"Thanks a million, Jeff." Steve cut in with a smile. Jeff straightened and left, closing the door quietly behind him. Then, as we fell on the food like hyenas, Steve turned to us again, looking so dang enthusiastic that I wondered how much coffee he'd had this morning. "So! You kids want to be big stars, eh?"

"God, no!" I said, almost spewing crumbs. "No way!"

Oddly, this seemed to throw a petite wrench into the convo.

4

SHARON AND STEVE and the other two agents went silent, looking at us in surprise.

Steve recovered quickly. "Models?" he suggested, his eyes noting that we were all tall and skinny for our age.

I almost snorted Sprite through my nose. "Yeah. 'Wings are being worn wide this year,'" I pretended to quote. "'With the primary feathers tinted fun shades of pink and green for a party look.' I don't think so." I tried not to notice Nudge's momentary disappointment.

"Actors?" Sharon said.

Total perked up, chewing busily on calamari, which, if you're interested, is Italian for rubber bands.

"Nope." I could see this interview was going south, so I started inhaling food while I could.

"Max, I mean—Max," Steve said, with no idea what else to call me. "You're selling yourself short. You guys could do anything, be anything. You want your own movie? You want flock action figures? You want to be on T-shirts? You name it, kid—I can make it happen."

"I want to be an action figure!" Gazzy said, wolfing down some mini-enchilada thingies.

"Oh, yeah!" Iggy said, holding up his hand for a high five. The Gasman slapped it.

Steve smiled and seemed to relax. "Hey, I didn't catch everyone's names. You, sweetheart," he said to Angel. "What's your name?"

"Isabella von Frankenstein Rothschild," said Angel, absently picking something out of her teeth. She'd lost one of her front ones recently, so her grin had a black hole in it. "You got your shoes on eBay," she told Sharon, whose eyes widened about as far as they could. "But you're right—it doesn't make sense to go retail, not on what Skinflint Steve pays you."

Yep, that's my little mind-readin' darlin'!

There was dead silence for a few moments. Sharon blushed hotly and looked anywhere but at Steve. One of the other agents coughed.

"Ah, huh," Steve said, then turned to Gazzy. "How about you, son? You want to be an action figure, right? What's your name?"

Gazzy nodded eagerly, and I promised myself I'd kick his butt later. "They call me the Sharkalator."

"The Sharkalator," Steve repeated, his enthusiasm waning. What can I say? We have that effect on grown-ups. Even on other kids. Well, okay, on pretty much everyone. We were created to survive, not to be the life of the party.

"I'm Cinnamon," said Nudge, licking her fingers. "Cinnamon Allspice La Fever. This shrimp is awesome."

Steve started to look depressed.

"They call me the White Knight," said Iggy, expertly finding the remaining food on the trays with his sensitive fingers.

"Oh?" Sharon said, trying to salvage the situation. "Why is that?"

Iggy looked in her general direction. He gestured to his pale blond hair, pale skin, unseeing blue eyes. "They're not gonna call me the *Black* Knight."

Fang had sat silently this whole time, so still that he was practically blending into the modern tufted sofa. He had drunk four Cokes in about four minutes and steadily worked his way through a plate of fried something-or-others. Now he felt all eyes turn to him, and he looked up, the expression on his face making me shiver.

No one looks like Fang—dark and still and dangerous, like he's daring you to set him off. But I'd seen him rocking Angel when she'd hurt herself; I'd seen him smile in his sleep; I'd seen the deep, dark light in his eyes as he leaned over me...

I blinked several times and chugged the rest of my Sprite.

Fang sighed and wiped his fingers on his black jeans. He looked around the whole room, at the four agents, at the younger kids having a ball with this, at Total slurping Fanta out of a bowl, at me, sitting tensely on the edge of my chair.

"My name is Fang," he said, standing up. "And I'm outta here." He walked to the sliding glass doors that led to a landscaped balcony, twenty-two stories above the ground.

I nodded at the flock and reached over to tap the back of Iggy's hand twice. He stood up and followed Fang's almost silent footsteps, weaving unerringly around tables and large potted plants.

Fang slid the door open. It was windy on the balcony, and he raised his face to the sun. I hustled the rest of the flock outside, then turned and waved lamely at the four open-mouthed, big-shot Hollywood agents.

"Thanks," I said, balancing on the balcony edge as my family took off one by one, leaping and unfurling their wings like soft, rough-edged sails, "but no thanks."

Then I threw myself out into the open air, feeling it rush through my hair, my feathers; feeling my wings buoy me up, every stroke lifting me twelve feet higher.

We're just not cut out for all this media circus crap.

But then, you already knew that.

5

"ALL I'M SAYING IS, would going on Oprah *just once* be the end of the entire world?" Nudge crossed her arms over her chest, glaring at me. Since Nudge is about the sweetest, easiest-going recombinant-DNA life-form I've ever known, this was serious.

"No," I said carefully. "But the end of the entire world would be the end of the *entire* world, and that's what we're still trying to stop." For those of you who are still catching up, I've been told that my mission in life is to save the world. No pressure or anything.

"I want to be an action figure," said Gazzy.

"Guys," I said, rubbing my temples, "remember four days ago? The bullets whizzing past, the sniper, the exploding building?"

"*I* certainly haven't forgotten." Total huffed, looking at his tail.

My pool of patience, never deep on the best of days, became yet shallower. "My point is," I went on tightly, "that clearly, someone is still after us, still wants us dead. Yes, our air shows for the CSM are big hits; there are people who are sort of accepting us as being... different, but we're still in danger. We'll *always* be in danger."

"I'm tired of being in danger!" Nudge cried. "I hate this! I just want to—"

She stopped, because there was no point in going on. Trying not to cry, she flopped down on the hotel bed. I sat down next to her and rubbed her back, between her wings.

"We all hate this," I said quietly. "But until someone can prove to me beyond a doubt that we're safe, I have to make decisions that will keep us more or less in one piece. I know it sucks."

"Speaking of things sucking," said Fang, "I say we ditch the air shows completely."

"I like the air shows," said Gazzy. He was lying on the floor, half beneath our coffee table. My mom had gotten him some little Transformer cars, and he was rolling them around, making engine noises. Yes, he could best most grown men in hand-to-hand combat and make an explosive device out of virtually anything, but he was still eight years old. Or so.

I always seemed to forget that.

"I like the air shows too," said Nudge, her tangly hair fanned out around her head. "They make me feel like a famous movie star."

"They're not safe," Fang said flatly.

I was torn. The sniper who had shot at me had turned out to be a new form of cyborg/human—or at least that's what we'd figured after we found part of one arm. Instead of a hand, he'd had an automatic pistol connected directly to his muscles and nerves. It hadn't actually been the building that exploded when we were close—it had been the sniper himself. He'd blown himself up rather than let us catch him or really see him.

That's dedication for ya.

That thing hadn't grafted that gun to his arm by himself. Someone had made him. That someone was still out there and possibly had made more things like him.

On the other hand...the CSM was really counting on us to continue the air shows. These shows were taking place in some of the most polluted cities in the world: Los Angeles, Sao Paulo, Moscow, Beijing. So far they'd been big successes, and the CSM had been able to hand out tons of cards and leaflets educating people about pollution and greenhouse gases.

My mom was a member of the CSM. She'd never want to put us in danger, but...I hated to let her down. She'd saved my life a bunch of times. She was helping the flock any way she could. This was the only thing she'd ever asked me to do. How could I tell her that I wanted to bail?

"Maybe if we just do the air shows but have them way step up security," I said slowly.

"No," said Fang.

Okay. I may be fabulous in a lot of ways, but I know I have a couple tiny flaws. One of them is a really bad knee-jerk reaction whenever anyone tells me no about anything.

You'd think Fang would have picked up on that by now.

I raised my chin and looked him in the eye. The flock, being smarter than the average gang of winged bears, went still.

Slowly, I stood up and walked closer to Fang. Out of the corner of my eye, I saw Total slither beneath a bed, saw Gazzy quickly pull Iggy into the boys' room next door.

Until last year, I'd been taller than both Fang and Iggy. They'd not only caught up but had shot several inches past me, which I hated. Now Fang looked down at me, his eyes so dark I couldn't see where his pupils were.

"What?" I asked, deceptively mildly. I saw a flash of pink tutu as Angel and Nudge crawled with quick, silent efficiency into the boys' room.

"The air shows are too dangerous," Fang said equally mildly. I heard the connecting door between the two rooms ease shut with the caution of prey trying hard not to attract its predator.

"I can't let my mom down." This close, I could see his thick eyelashes, the weird glints of gold in his eyes.

He let out a breath slowly and clenched his hands.

"One more show," I offered.

His hands unclenched as he weighed his options. "All right," he said, surprising me. "You're right—we don't want to let the CSM down."

I looked at him in narrow-eyed suspicion, and then it hit me: Dr. Brigid Dwyer, the eighth wonder of the world, was part of the CSM. She'd planned on meeting us in Mexico City, our next show.

That was why Fang had agreed to just one more—so he could get all caught up with his favorite brilliant, underage scientist.

I walked stiffly to the bathroom, locked the door, and turned on the shower as hard as it could go. Then I buried my face in a fluffy towel and shrieked like a banshee.

6

I'M NOT a great sleeper. When you've spent your whole life facing imminent pain and death, you tend not to sink too deeply into the arms of Morpheus. So it was nothing new that I lay awake for hours that night, turning this way and that.

I know what you're thinking: how do the wings fit into the whole sleeping thing? Well, even though our wings fold up pretty neatly and tightly along our spines, we're generally not back sleepers. We're mostly side or stomach sleepers. Little bit of insider bird-kid info for ya there.

Right now I was flopped on my stomach, my head hanging off the side of the bed I was sharing with Angel. Nudge won the Flock Member Most Likely to Cause Injuries by

Kicking During Sleep award last year, so she got a bed to herself.

My wings were unfolded a bit, and I reached around to pull a twig out of my secondaries. Here's what I was thinking about:

1) Who this new threat was
2) The air show in Mexico City
3) My mom and my half-sister, Ella
4) How to get Total to quit milking his tail injury, because enough was enough
5) Fang
6) Fang
7) Fang

I've grown up with Fang, from the very beginning, when our dog crates were stacked next to each other in the lab of experimental horror that we called the School. I know, just another typical romantic story about the boy next door.

Then we'd been rescued by our bad guy, turned good guy, turned bad again, turned I don't know what lately—and Fang and I had been like brother and sister with the rest of the flock, hidden away in the Colorado mountains.

Then Jeb (see description above) disappeared, and I became flock leader. Maybe because I was the oldest. Or the most ruthless. Or the most organized. I don't know.

But I was the flock leader, and Fang was my right-wing man.

This past year, things had started to change. Fang had been interested in a girl (see Red-Haired Wonder, book two), and I'd hated it. I'd had my first date with a guy (possibly evil, not sure), and Fang had hated it. Then, last month, he'd gotten all cozy with Dr. Brigid Dwyer, the twenty-year-old scientist who'd been part of the research team down in the land of ice and snow and killer leopard seals. And—get this—she'd sort of flirted back with him. And he's—practically—just a kid!

In the midst of all this, Fang had kissed me. Several times. So now I was freaked and tempted and terrified and worried and longing—and also angry at him for even starting this whole thing to begin with. But it was started and couldn't be unstarted. (Again, his fault.)

And now I was trying to brush my hair, you know, when I thought about it, and looking at myself in mirrors, wondering if I was pretty. Pretty! A year ago, when my hair got in my eyes, I hacked it off with a knife. The only thing important about my clothes was whether they were too stiff with *whatever* to move fast in battle. And Fang had been my best friend and an excellent fighter.

Now everything was upside down.

"You *are* really pretty, Max," said a small voice next to me.

I pressed my face into my pillow and squelched some extracolorful words. Way to go, ace—have embarrassing personal thoughts while you're *two feet* from a *mind reader.*

Yes. Along with the wings and the raptor eyesight and the weird bones, the insane scientists who'd created us had given us the potential to suddenly develop other skills. Iggy can feel colors. Nudge can draw metal stuff toward her and hack any computer. Fang can pretty much disappear into whatever background he's near. Gazzy can imitate any voice, any sound, with 100 percent accuracy. His other skill is unmentionable. I can fly faster than the others, and I have a Voice in my head. I don't want to talk about that right now.

But it was Angel who'd hit the genetic jackpot. She can breathe under water, communicate with fish, and read people's minds. We're talking about a six-year-old. And, you know, six-year-olds are *famous* for having excellent *judgment* and *decision-making skills.*

"You have nice hair and really pretty eyes," Angel went on earnestly.

I rolled over a bit. "Yeah. Brown and brown." Have I mentioned how much Fang loves *red* hair? I believe I have.

"No, your hair has little sun streaks in it," Angel informed me. "And your eyes are like—you know those chocolates we had in France? With the gooey stuff in the middle, with the alcohol in 'em except we didn't know, and Gazzy ate a million and then barfed all night? Those chocolates?"

As much as I had tried to suppress all memory of that incident, it rushed back to me in vivid Technicolor. "The color of my eyes is like barfed-up chocolate?" Despair settled over me. There was no hope.

"No, the chocolates before they were barfed," Angel clarified.

So there you have it, the extent of my charms: brown hair and eyes like unbarfed chocolate. I'm a lucky girl.

"Max," said Angel. "You know Fang is the best guy ever. And he loves you. 'Cause you're the best girl ever."

With anyone else, I could ask them how they know that and then discredit them. Not Angel. She knew because she'd seen it, in his mind.

"We all love each other, Ange," I said impatiently, hating this whole conversation.

"No, not like this," she went on relentlessly. "Fang loves you."

Here's a little secret you might not have picked up on about me: I can't stand gushy emotion. Hate crying. Hate feeling sad. Am not even too crazy about feeling happy. So all this—the vulnerability, the longing, the terror—I desperately wanted it to all go away forever. I wanted to cut it out of me like they'd cut out that chip. (See book three; I can't keep explaining everything. If I'm gonna take the trouble to write this stuff down, the least you can do is read it.)

But right now, I needed Angel to shut up.

"Okay, maybe I'll give him a break," I said, rolling over and closing my eyes.

"Maybe you should give him more than that," Angel pressed.

My eyes flared open as I didn't dare to think what she might mean.

"He could totally be your boyfriend," she went on with annoying persistence. "You guys could get married. I could be like a junior bridesmaid. Total could be your flower dog."

"I'm only a kid!" I shrieked. "I can't get married!"

"You could in New Hampshire."

My mouth dropped open. How does she know this stuff? "Forget it! No one's getting married!" I hissed. "Not in New Hampshire or anywhere else! Not in a box, not with a fox! Now go to sleep, *before I kill you!*"

Oh yeah, like I got any sleep after *that*.

7

YOU'VE NEVER SEEN just how mega a megalopolis can be until you've seen Mexico City. I guess there might be bigger burgs in like China or something, but boy howdy, Mexico City seems endless.

Anyway, the Bane of My Existence and I had agreed to one more air show, and of course it was the one in Mexico City, where Dr. Wonderful would be meeting us.

So we were over a ginormous open-air stadium, the Estadio Azteca, which held about 114,000 people. Every seat was filled. We'd changed the choreography and order of stunts since the last show, so if anyone had made a plan to take us out, they'd have to rethink it. Around us, mile upon mile of densely packed buildings stretched as far as we could see, and we can see pretty dang far.

"I need a scuba tank," Nudge said, flying over to me. She was holding her nose with one hand. "And a face mask." She gave a couple of coughs and shook her head, her eyes watering.

"I assume you're referring to the wee pollution problem?" I said, raising my voice to be heard over the wind and the multitudes cheering below. The people in the stadium were looking up to see us silhouetted against a thick gray sky. But it was not a cloudy day. The thing is, with nineteen million-plus people and four million-plus cars and a bunch of businesses making stuff, Mexico City is incredibly, horribly, nauseatingly polluted.

Which was why the CSM wanted us to be there—to bring international attention to it. When Dr. Wonderful was prepping us for the air show, she'd told us that there had been half a million pollution-related hospital cases just in the past year.

Now we were wondering if we were going to raise that number to half a million and seven.

"I'm getting a headache," Gazzy said, circling closer to me. We split apart in a six-pointed star, with Total in the middle, and the crowd below went crazy. Like a huge, rolling wave of sound, the chants came to us.

"We have the power! The future is now! Kids rule!"

I raised an eyebrow at Fang. "Kids rule?"

He shrugged. "I can't control what they quote from the blog," he said. "What am I gonna say? 'More power to grown-ups?' I don't think so."

"How many readers do you have now?" Fang had started a blog months ago, using our super-duper-contraband computer. He had his own fan clubs and everything. Girls sent him ridiculous e-mails about how wonderful he was, what a hero, etc. It was enough to turn your stomach.

"About six hundred thousand log in pretty much every day," Fang said, automatically scanning the airspace around us. He and I suddenly soared upward, facing each other, about two feet apart. The crowd below gasped, and I knew it looked impressive as all get-out.

Then Iggy zoomed up to join us, and he, Fang, and I made a triangle, our wings moving in perfect order so that we didn't whap each other on the upstroke. Total hovered way above us, like a star on top of a Christmas tree.

A hundred yards below us, Nudge, Gazzy, and Angel were a triple stack of bird kids, centered one over the other, moving their wings in unison: everyone up, everyone down. At Gazzy's signal, they all turned and started rocketing earthward, still precisely stacked.

Fang, Iggy, Total, and I counted to ten, then angled downward also: it was time for us to land on the field. Supposedly they were going to give us some kind of award.

"You're national heroes," Dr. Amazing had said earlier, pushing her, yes, *red* hair out of her eyes while Fang watched her with interest. "Not only here, but in other countries too. You guys are so young, but you've accomplished so much and exposed so much evil. Plus, you helped publicize the melting of the planet's ice, and spoke to Congress. You're amazing."

Who was she beaming at? Yes. Fang.

Who, exactly, had gotten up the nerve to speak to Congress? That would be *moi*.

But, judging from Brigid Dwyer's unprofessional adoration, Fang alone had just saved the entire known world with one wing tied behind his back.

It had been all I could do not to trip Brigid on her way out. Which was stupid, because why did I care? Never mind. Forget I asked.

The field below—big enough for the World Cup, the Olympics, and anything else where 114,000 people suddenly needed to be at the same place at the same time—beckoned us. There was a line of uniformed security guards hired by the CSM ringing the perimeter to protect us.

I saw Nudge, Gazzy, and Angel land flawlessly and wave at the crowd as a hundred thousand cameras flashed. Unfortunately, since a camera flash bears a striking resemblance to the flash a gun makes when it's fired, by the time I reached the ground, I was so twitchy and pumped full of adrenaline that I felt like I might hurl.

We joined the rest of the flock on the green turf and then all automatically circled, facing outward, as if we were six (and a half) cute little covered wagons warding off Indians who were inexplicably ticked off that we'd taken all their land and given them colds and killed most of them.

The crowd was roaring too loudly for us to hear guns. Heck, we wouldn't have been able to hear a chopper. It was, pretty much, the most nightmarish situation I could possibly imagine, without literally involving a dog crate.

And you know what's coming, right?

Yeah. The actual nightmare part.

8

The setting: An impossibly big open stadium in impressive but noxious Mexico City.
The cast of characters: The flock, Total, Dr. Amazing, and some very nice Mexican officials who wanted to give us an award. Plus a TV crew.
The plot: Just wait. It's coming.

"I hate this. Get me outta here," I said to Fang, keeping a smile stuck to my face. We were waving to the crowd, so many camera flashes going off that I was sure I'd be blind in a minute.

"This is not a good setup," Fang agreed, looking around constantly.

Total, Iggy, Gazzy, and Nudge were working the crowd

like old hands, bowing and soaking up the applause. Gazzy was spreading his wings and doing little six-foot hops into the air, and each time the crowd roared even louder.

Finally, one of the assembled officials tapped on a microphone located at the center of the stadium. Brigid Dwyer stood next to them, ready to give a speech about the CSM and what it was trying to accomplish worldwide.

The official said something in Spanish, and the crowd cheered and clapped, chanting quotes from Fang's blog. Then Brigid took the microphone and waited for relative quiet.

"*Buenos días, señors y señoras*," Brigid said, and people cheered. "*Hoy nosotros*—"

Right then, a piercing scream soared above the crowd's murmur and stopped Brigid cold. Gazzy saw them first: ninja-type thingies leaping over the upper ledge of the stadium and rappelling down to the field.

"Heads up!" Fang shouted. We had a second to exchange glances, thinking the same thing: We hadn't seen them on the roof, just minutes before. Where had they come from?

"Up and away!" I yelled to the flock, then saw the problem: Brigid couldn't fly out with us. We couldn't leave her to the ninjas' mercy, or lack thereof. We couldn't abandon her and the rest of the people who had hosted us.

The officials, Brigid, and the TV crew gazed open-mouthed as at least sixty slim, dark figures hit the ground and headed for us. I sized up the situation in an instant: a hundred thousand people who might be injured or killed in crossfire; innocent people right here on the field who would only get in our way; the seven of us up against about sixty of whatever this new threat was.

It was like old times.

"Belay that!" I shouted. "Battle up!"

As a maternal figure, I always try to keep the flock safe, of course. But I admit, it did my heart proud to see the instant blood-lust pop into Gazzy's blue eyes and to see little Angel automatically tense up and get into fighting stance, ready to rip someone's head off. They were just so—so dang *adorable,* sometimes.

We were a tiny bit out of practice. I hadn't taken anyone apart in several weeks. But once you've learned the nasty, street-fighting, no-holds-barred art of Max Kwon Do, you never really forget it.

"Get 'em!" I shouted as the dark figures raced toward us. Liquid-fire adrenaline surged into my veins, making me jittery and lightning fast.

As soon as one was within striking range, I jumped up and out, both feet forward. They connected heavily, slamming the New Threat in its middle. It doubled over but snapped upright quickly, its dark hood slipping back to reveal a weird, humanish face. Humanish except for the glowing green laserlike eyes.

I landed, spun on one heel, and snapkicked backward as hard as I could. I caught it in the shoulder and heard a crunching, breaking sound.

With its good arm, it swung at my head, much faster than a human could and with more force. I leaped backward just in time, feeling the barest brush of its knuckles against my cheek.

A second one rushed up, followed by a third. One grabbed me from behind, tearing my jacket—my new jacket that my mom had given me. Brand-new, not from Goodwill or a Dumpster. He'd *torn* it.

Now I was mad. A split-second glance revealed that the flock was doing what it did best: deconstructing things. No one needed help, so I balled my fists, put my head down, and went after my attackers.

These skirmishes always seem to last much longer than they actually do. I felt like I was punching and kicking and swinging and whaling for two hours, but it was probably about six minutes or so. During that time, I figured out that these New Threat thingies had a couple vulnerable spots: If you brought both hands down in a chopping motion right on top of their heads, their heads actually split open into several metallic strips, like a sectioned orange. Okay, a really gross orange, but you get the idea.

Another vulnerable spot: their trim little ankles. One good strong kick, and they snapped like balsa wood.

In less than ten minutes, thanks to us and the hired security force, the grassy lawn looked like a combination of an army field hospital and an automobile chop shop. Brigid and the officials were white-faced, huddled together by the podium. A quick inventory of the flock revealed the usual bruises, bloody noses, and black eyes, but nothing serious.

Fang came up to me, his face grim, his knuckles raw and bleeding.

I knew what he was going to say. "Okay. No more air shows," I said.

9

DR. DWYER AND THE CSM had arranged for a special safe house for us—actually five, four were decoys—and kept the real location a secret until we were in a car headed there.

"Seeing battles is hard, if you're not used to it," Fang said, watching Brigid's white face. She nodded tensely, struggling to maintain her cool. She hadn't been hurt, but her clothes were spattered with blood—I'd been standing right next to her when I had happily discovered the New Threat's orangey weakness.

"It's not a picnic even if you *are* used to it," I said.

"What were those things?" Iggy asked, rubbing his bruised and scraped knuckles.

"Not sure," I said. I'd been trying to figure that out myself. They hadn't been Erasers, those wolf-human hybrids that had tried to kill us about once every hour for the last four years. They hadn't been Flyboys, which were the flying, cyborg version of Erasers. They hadn't been straight robots. They were roboty, but with a bit of flesh grown over their frames, and apparently didn't fly. They hadn't spoken, but that didn't mean they couldn't.

"It's a mystery," I said, deciding to worry about it later. Right now I was hungry and a little shaky from the drop in adrenaline.

I pushed my hair out of my eyes, and just then noticed that Dr. Brilliant's hair was actually cut in a style, like on *purpose*. I've had my hair cut by an actual hairdresser exactly once in my life, and that was many, many battles ago.

I felt like a truck driver next to Brigid Dwyer. A truck driver with bad hair, a black eye, dried blood around my nose, and ripped and bloody clothes. Not an unusual look for me, but all of a sudden, I felt—I don't know. I don't know what I felt.

"Here we are," said Brigid as we pulled into the driveway of a smallish stucco house. The houses were packed tightly together here, and the streets were full of dogs and cars, the yards strung with lines of clean laundry.

I automatically scanned the area for possible hiding places, points of vulnerability, whether the windows were breakable, whether the trees would get in our way. Fang got out first, raked the area with his stare, and determined that it was safe.

The rest of us piled out quickly and hurried to the back of the house. I felt tired and irritable and, worse, kept sensing Brigid looking at Fang. I just wanted to eat about three banana splits and then collapse.

Warm yellow light spilled out a window, forming a slanted rectangle on the grass. Just as we reached the back door, it swung open. I stopped so suddenly that Angel bumped into me. I got on the balls of my feet, ready to leap into action if someone dangerous was behind that door.

At first all I saw was a silhouette. At the same moment, a delicious, familiar scent wafted out into the warm night air.

Chocolate chip cookies, fresh from the oven.

The silhouette was my mom, Dr. Valencia Martinez, and she was smiling at me.

And the world seemed loads better.

10

"MAN, I FEEL GREAT," Gazzy said an hour later. He tipped back in his chair and patted his stomach, now full of enchiladas, tacos, chips and salsa, and cookies. "Looove Mexico," he crooned. "Looove Mexican food."

"It's so good to see you again," my mom said, kissing my cheek. Again.

I beamed at her. "You too. And I haven't seen Ella in ages."

"I've got so much to tell you," my half sister said to me. She quickly pushed a couple tortilla chips into her mouth, her eyes wide. "We had a dance at my school!"

My mom smiled at Ella, looking tired and proud. "Yes, she even gave up two hours with me to attend. Ella and I have been stuffing envelopes and making phone calls for the CSM in every spare minute."

For a second I was jealous—Ella had so much more of my mom, all the time, her whole life. Then I felt guilty. Ella deserved to have our mom, and it wasn't her fault that I couldn't. The fact was, my mom had had Ella in the normal way. I had been an egg donated to science and was fertilized in a test tube. Neither of us knew the other existed until this past year. And now, no matter how much we cared about each other, it was still too dangerous for me to live in one place for any length of time. Being with my mom would also mean putting her and Ella at risk. And I wouldn't do it.

Amazingly, I'm not that selfish. Yet.

"You've been doing an incredible job for the CSM too, honey," my mom said to me. "But I agree that the air shows must be canceled. There's just no way to guarantee your safety."

Jeb Batchelder pulled out a chair and sat down, propping his elbows on the table and lacing his fingers together. "Has everyone had enough to eat?" he asked.

I slowly let out a breath, not looking at him. I would never get used to seeing him again, after thinking he was dead for years. I would never accept that he was a good guy, after everything he'd done to me and the flock over the last—what was it now? Eight months? Time was so—stretchy, in my life.

Somehow my mom trusted him. And I trusted my mom. But that was as far as it went, despite the fact that as far as I knew, he was my biological father, the other half of the test-tube cocktail that had produced me. But I never, ever thought of him as my father. Ever.

"The CSM isn't our only concern right now," Jeb said. His hair was starting to go gray. I'd love to think that I caused some of it. "We need to discuss your next steps."

Instantly I felt my face set like stone. I didn't look at Fang but knew that he'd have the same expression. None of us had ever reacted well to the amusing notion of having grown-ups decide things for us—like our future, or what we did, and so on.

"Oh?" I said in a voice that would have made most people pause.

Jeb was used to it, having heard it from me since I was about three years old.

"Yes," he said. "A new school was recently created—the Day and Night School. It's for gifted children, and it's designed to let kids learn at their natural pace, in ways that suit them best. You'd all do really well there. It's one of the only schools on earth where you'd fit in."

"Yeah, we're all about fitting in," I said, rolling my eyes.

"Where is it?" Nudge asked. I heard the eagerness in her voice, and groaned to myself.

"In a beautiful and secluded part of Utah," Jeb said. "It's got mountains, a lake to swim in, and horses to ride."

"Ooh," said Nudge, her brown eyes wide. "I love horses! And school—" A wistful expression came over her face. "Tons of books, and other kids to talk to..."

"Nudge, it's out of the question," I said. I hated to rain on her parade, but she knew this was crazy. There was no way we could go to some school somewhere. Had she forgotten what had happened the other times we'd tried to go to school? It was like, regular usual nightmare, plus homework.

Nudge turned pleading eyes to me. "Really? It would be nice to be in one place for a while, and learn things."

"I like school," said Ella. "Even though some kids are buttheads."

"We usually have bigger problems than kids being buttheads," I said, trying to squelch my growing irritation. "Nudge, you know we have to keep on the move. Remember the suicide-sniper guy? There's no way we'd be safe."

"We can guarantee your safety," Jeb offered. "This is the real deal, kids."

"Oh, the real deal," I said, sarcasm dripping. "So it's better than all the fake deals, huh? Guarantee our safety? Please. How can you even say that with a straight face?"

"I've checked into it," my mom said. "I have to admit, it seems like a good program. And the woman who runs it is one of my friends from college."

Well, Buddha himself could come to me in a dream and tell me it was the right thing to do, and I still would not get on board. Because when it comes right down to it, in the end, when push comes to shove, when my back's against the wall, when I can't think of another freaking cliché to throw your way, the only person I really, really, really trust, no matter what, is me.

This policy has paid off for me any number of times.

The next person I trust after me is Fang.

There really isn't a third person, not because I don't love the flock or my mom or whoever, but because Fang is the only person I know almost as well as I know myself, and he's the only person I know who is close to being as tough as I am. He will not break under torture; he will not sell me out.

So, on various levels of trust after Fang, I'd choose the rest of the flock, my mom, and Ella. Jeb didn't make the list.

"School is out," I said firmly. "Next question."

11

DO YOU WANT TO KNOW what's the closest thing to feeling the most powerful you can feel? Flying alone at night. Risky. Nothing but you and the wind. Soaring way above everything, slicing through the air like a sword. Up and up until you feel like you could grab a star and hold it to your chest like a burning, spiky thing...

Oh, the poetry of a bird kid. Remind me to collect it all into one emotional, mushy volume someday, under some fake, poetic-sounding name, like Gabrielle Charbonnet de la Something-Schmancy. (I'm not kidding. I saw that name on a backpack in France. Poor kid.)

I wheeled through the sky, racing as fast as I could, my wings moving like pistons, up and down, strong and sleek. When I felt an updraft of warmer air, I coasted, breathing in the night's thin coolness, dipping a wing to turn in huge, smooth circles as big as football fields.

Breathe in, breathe out.

Everyone was back at the house, asleep, I hoped. I'd sneak in before anyone woke up and saw I was gone and freaked out and thought I'd been kidnapped or something. But right now I needed some time. Some space. Some breathing room.

Once again, the fate of the flock was in my hands, and once again, I seemed to be the only one seeing or thinking clearly enough to know that there really wasn't even a choice here. School was *never* actually a real choice.

Why didn't the rest of the flock ever see that?

We're the flock. We're the last, most successful, still-living recombinant life-form that the Dr. Frankenstein wannabes at the School had created. That pretty much cemented us to one road in life, one fate: to run—forever.

Why did the rest of the flock keep pretending that we had choices? It was a waste of time. Worse, it was always up to me to be the bad guy, the one who shot down everyone's hopes and dreams. You think I liked being the heavy? I didn't.

Breathe in, breathe out.

And Fang. He usually supported me. Which I appreciated. But lately he'd been lobbying for us to find a deserted island somewhere and just kick back, eat coconuts, and chill, without anyone knowing where we were.

Sometimes that sounded really good.

But how long could that last? Sooner or later, Nudge was going to want new shoes, or Gazzy would run out of comic books, or Angel would decide she wanted to rule the world, and then where would we be?

Right. We'd be back to me telling everyone no.

And Fang. I didn't know what he was doing, kissing me and then flirting with Dr. Stupendous and then making hot, dark eyes at me.

It was enough to make a girl nuts or *more* nuts—

Pssshh!

It took several seconds for the pain neurons to fire all the way from my right wing to my befuddled brain. And since I was conditioned to try not to scream out in surprise or pain—it's a survival thing—I was still staring stupidly at the weirdly big hole even as I started to spiral awkwardly down to earth, *way* too fast.

I'd been shot. I was plummeting to the ground. And I couldn't stop.

12

FOR THOSE OF YOU studying animal physiology, I'll confirm that there's a very good reason flying creatures always have two wings. One wing doesn't cut it.

By the time I'd processed what had happened, I was about ten seconds from a flat, crunchy death. I sent all available power into my unharmed wing and desperately tried to get some lift, managing to look like a dying loon, rising awkwardly a few feet, then sinking, all the while spiraling down like one of those copter toys.

This was it. After everything I'd ever been through, I was going to die suddenly, with no warning, and alone. I'm a tough kid, but I'll admit, I closed my eyes when I was about thirty feet from the asphalt of some parking lot.

I felt sorry for whoever would find me. I hoped the

flock would know I was dead and not just missing, so they wouldn't have to look for me. I thought about everything I had left unsaid to virtually everyone in my life, and wondered whether that had been a good—

Boing!

"Aiiiieee!!!!"

Interestingly, though I'm silent as the grave when shot or snuck up on, I discovered that I squeal like a little girl when I'm facing imminent death and then find myself bouncing hard on a trampoline.

The impact jolted my hurt wing, making me wince and suck in a breath, and then I was bouncing again, not so high, and again. I pulled my injured wing in tight, feeling warm, sticky blood clotting my feathers.

A couple more bounces and I managed to stand up, looking around me wildly. There were about a hundred of the New Threat guys, standing around the trampoline, watching me bounce, as if I were a mouse and they were all cats, honing in on me with bright eyes.

"Mr. Chu wants to see you," one of them intoned in a telephone operator's static voice.

They tipped me off the trampoline and immediately surrounded me, eight deep, not taking any chances. I couldn't fly. There were too many of them for me to realistically break free. This is probably how most humans feel all the time.

It sucks.

13

I WAS PUSHED into the back of a truck, fenced in by so many armed guards that I couldn't see anything.

My family had no idea where I was.

My right wing had a big hole in it, and one of its bones was probably broken.

I was completely outnumbered, going who knew where, to meet my mysterious new enemy, "Mr. Chu."

I decided to take a nap.

"Excuse me, pardon me," I murmured, sinking to my knees. Many of the guards immediately hunched down next to me, waiting for the daring escape I'd make by, what, slithering out between their legs?

Instead, I pushed and shouldered and kneed these things away and curled up on my left side, keeping my injured wing carefully on top. It hurt like heck, a throbbing, burning pain that reminded me with every beat of my heart that I couldn't fly.

The guards didn't know what to make of this. I guessed they hadn't been programmed to shrug their shoulders or make a "Whatever" face.

They weren't Erasers. They weren't Flyboys. They weren't the increasingly advanced robot soldiers that the diabolical brains-on-a-stick criminal known as the Uber-Director had created.

Heck, I didn't know what they were. Just—killing machines with delicate heads and ankles. Kind of geeky. Machine geeks. Hey! M-Geeks.

Good. Now they had a name, at least in my head.

I was very tired. And I went to sleep.

14

"I TOLD YOU she was not to be killed!"

The harsh, strongly accented voice filtered into my drowsy ears. The next thing I was aware of was the pain in my wing. It hurt so much that I wanted to cry. Or at least whimper loudly.

"It is not dead," said an M-Geek. I loved that name. "It is... limp."

These things had been given quite the vocab.

"She's bloody."

"We shot it to get it out of the sky."

Okay, so it wasn't lilting poetry, but it was leagues ahead of chess-playing computers.

As much fun as it was to listen to them talking about

me like I wasn't there, I decided time was a-wasting. I opened my eyes and coughed.

I was on a blanket on a floor. The floor was shifting subtly in a way I immediately recognized: I was on a boat. I got to my feet, trying to keep from shrieking in pain.

Standing before me was an Asian man, a couple inches shorter than me, but then I'm weirdly tall. He was stocky and wore glasses and the kind of plain, navy Chinese jacket you see in old movies. Thick black hair was brushed back severely from his face.

"Maximum Ride," he said, not holding out his hand. "I am Mr. Chu."

"What do you want, Mr. Chu?" Might as well cut right to the chase.

"I want to explain to you that you must immediately sever your ties to the Coalition to Stop the Madness," the man said, looking intently into my eyes.

That couldn't be all. "And?" I prompted.

"You do not know what they are really up to," he went on. "They are just using you to promote their own agenda."

"They're paying us in doughnuts," I felt compelled to point out.

"I represent a group of very powerful, very wealthy businessmen from around the world," said Mr. Chu.

"Of course you do," I said soothingly, trying to look for an exit without being too obvious.

"We are the only ones who really know what is going on."

"Of course you are."

There was a tiny skylight. Could I—oh. Max no fly. Bummer.

"There is an apocalypse coming," said Mr. Chu, seeming to grow more and more agitated.

"You're not the first person who's told me that."

"It is true! My group will survive the apocalypse. We are the only ones who will not become extinct after the world leaders succeed in their quest to destroy one another."

"Kinda makes you wish you were a world leader yourself, huh," I said sympathetically.

Smack!

My lightning-fast reflexes had let me whip my head to one side as he lunged forward, but he still gave me a good clip on the cheek. Slowly I straightened, feeling my cheek burn, my rage growing.

"You stupid, arrogant girl." He almost spit. "If you and your flock will join our group, then you will not be hunted down and destroyed. We can use you on our team. But if you keep up with the wisecracks and your stupidity, you will soon be eliminated. There will be no room for you in the new world."

"Again, not new information," I snarled, my fists clenched at my side. "The flock and I aren't for sale, Chuey. So all I can say is, Bring it!"

I braced for all of them to leap on me, steel-hard fists

adding to Mr. Chu's unconvincing argument. Instead, the man leaned closer. He smelled of cigarettes.

"I am sorry that you and the flock will be dead soon. But my scientists will enjoy taking you apart to find out what makes you tick."

"If your scientists take me apart," I said solemnly, "clearly, I won't be ticking anymore."

Mr. Chu was practically steaming with anger, but he stuck to his script. "You may think I am dreaming, but I am not. What I say is true. It is as real as the pain in your wing and on your face. And speaking of pain, Maximum... you should know that we are experts in the art of persuasion."

"Pain fades," I said slowly. "But being a nutcase seems to stick around. Guess who got the better deal here?"

The last thing I remember is Mr. Chu's face blazing with fury.

15

I AM A BONA FIDE, kick-butt warrior, so it was pretty humiliating to be shoved out of a fast-moving car about half a mile from the safe house. I landed on my hurt wing, *of course,* and winced as I rolled to a crumpled stop.

My hands were bound behind my back. I got to my knees as soon as I could, then to my feet, feeling shaky and ill. My wing was streaked with clotted blood. I was light-headed and starving. My face hurt, and my cheek was swollen and warm.

The flock and I all have an acute, innate sense of direction, so after a minute I turned and started trotting east. Once I reached the safe house, I headed for the back door, which was locked, *of course,* because I had gone out through a second-story window hours before. My plan to be all sneaky so that no one would notice I was missing had been blown to heck. Sighing, I turned around and headed for the front door.

This whole sucky episode ended with my having to actually *ring the doorbell* at the front of the house with my shoulder. Total even barked like a real dog. A curtain twitched, and then my mom opened the door, her brown eyes wide.

My mom is a veterinarian, an animal doctor, so let's all put our hands together for the irony there. She patched my wing while she and Jeb tried unsuccessfully to find out what had happened. I wanted to mull things over for a while, maybe do some research on the Chu-ster, so I just mumbled something about getting hit by a stray bullet in a freak accident.

"You shouldn't fly for at least a week," my mom said firmly.

I instantly interpreted that to mean three days.

"And I really mean a week," she went on, looking stern. "Not three days."

She was getting to know me.

Later that day, the CSM moved us to another house, this time in the Yucatan, which is a jungley part of Mexico. There weren't as many people there, and the air was much more breathable, with less texture.

But what did the air quality matter, anyway? I couldn't fly.

Me being unable to fly is not only my worst nightmare, but everyone else's too, because I turn into such a cranky witch. By the afternoon of the first day, the flock was staying out of my way. They went out and did flocklike things. Total was practicing his takeoffs and landings, both of which he still sucked at.

I warned them to be careful, to be on guard, not to stay out too long. They were fine. Had no problems. Did not get shot at. Did not get kidnapped and taken to see a short, angry Asian man.

I stayed home and was forced to heal.

"Jeb," I said, speaking to him voluntarily for the first time in ages. He smiled and raised his eyebrows at me. "Have you ever heard of a Mr. Chu?"

The blood seemed to drain from his face, and I saw him struggle to keep a calm expression. "No," he said slowly, shaking his head. "Can't say that I have. Where did you hear that name?"

I shrugged and walked away. He'd given me all the answer I needed.

Later I watched my flock fly away without me, off to have loads of bird-kid fun.

"Max."

"What?" I snarled, turning from the window.

My mom stood there. I felt a little bad about snarling.

"Come on. I'm going to show you how to make Puchero Yucateco." She gently pulled me away from the window.

Please don't let this be a craft, I prayed silently. *If she pulls out yarn, I'll—*

As it turns out, Puchero Yucateco is a stew made with three kinds of meat.

Me, my mom, and Ella spent all afternoon in the kitchen, chopping up things, stirring, mixing. My mom showed us how to tell when onions had cooked enough to be sweet, and how to tell when meat was done (usually I just try to wait for it to stop moving). We cut up habanero peppers, and despite all her warnings, I managed to brush my finger against my nose, so my nose burned and ran, and my eyes watered, and I staggered around the kitchen going "Uh, uh, uh!" while Ella collapsed with laughter.

Typical family stuff. With a nonflock family.

"Huh—why is Max in the kitchen?" Gazzy asked as he walked in. His face was flushed, hair permanently tousled from the wind. Clearly he'd been having a glorious, exhilarating time, coasting high above the world. And wasn't that *special* for him.

"We're cooking," said my mom.

"She's just keeping you company, right?" he asked nervously as my eyes narrowed. Nudge, Fang, Iggy, Angel, and Total all crammed into the kitchen and stared at the wooden spoon in my hand.

"No," my mom replied, trying to keep a straight face. "She's cooking."

Quick, alarmed glances were exchanged among the flock.

"Cooking...food?" Nudge asked. I heard someone murmur something about ordering a pizza.

"Yes, I'm cooking food, and it's great, and you're going to eat it, you twerps!" I snapped.

And that was how I spent my three days of forced rest. The flock saw all the Mayan wonders of the Yucatan, and I learned how to cook something besides cold cereal.

So there was much amazement all around.

But my wing healed, and soon it was time to leave. I was thinking of maybe going to South America.

But the flock had different ideas. While I was healing, they'd taken a vote.

They wanted to try Jeb's Day and Night School.

16

"WE STILL HAVE NO SIGHTINGS of the girl Maximum Ride," reported one scout.

The team leader glanced up from the radar images on his desk. "What about the others?"

"We've been tracking them for three days," his subordinate confirmed. "We've triangulated their origination point to within a half mile."

The team leader looked up, but his frown was lost on the combat robot, who hadn't been upgraded to recognize emotion.

"What's the fastest they were clocked at?" he asked.

"The large dark one can achieve speeds of more than two hundred fifty miles per hour," said the scout. "When they are aiming downward, they have been recorded at more than three hundred fifty miles per hour."

The team leader nodded, wondering why the upgrade also apparently hadn't been programmed to use metric. He sighed. The history of these genetic mistakes was a litany of embarrassing failures. Even Itexicon—with its massive, global resources, the years of research, the trillions of dollars spent—had ended up a shattered shell, unable to stop six children. And the Erasers! People were still making jokes about them.

When he'd first heard about the Erasers, he'd thought they were simply an amusing experiment. Despite their speed, relative intelligence, and overwhelming bloodlust, they'd proved quite ineffective. So they'd decided to dispense with the biological base and went to robots covered with flesh—inexplicably designed to look like Erasers. Then they'd made Flyboys—basically, Erasers with wings. All of which the mutant kids had already defeated.

Since then, it had been basically the same old, same old—one generation of enhanced individual tracking and killing machines after the next. Given all kinds of fancy names, tweaked this way and that. None of them seemed up to the task.

The team leader was truly surprised that Devin had failed. Truly, truly surprised. Devin had never failed at a job for as long as the team leader had known him. He'd lost a hundred dollars on that bet.

However, there did seem to be a sufficient quantity of

version 5.0 to perhaps stall or contain the mutated kids until someone better, smarter, more experienced, more focused came along.

Someone like him.

"Should we pinpoint their location and destroy them?" the robot asked.

The team leader shook his head. "No. Just surveillance at this point."

He'd lost a bunch of good men in Mexico City, and he wanted payback.

So did Mr. Chu.

17

MY DAY:

1) Back in America. In one of the western states with all the ninety-degree angles.
2) Wing still messed up; perhaps need longer than three days till it's fully functional.
3) Had to say good-bye to Mom and Ella. Many mushy tears, soggy hugs. All that stuff I love.
4) Strong sense of betrayal by flock about Day and Night School. But without a 100 percent fly-ready wing, I couldn't soar off in a huff the way I wanted to.
5) Fang has hardly spoken to me for three days. He doesn't seem mad—more like thoughtful. Watching me. What is on his freaking mind?!

"School, school, school," Nudge sang as she got ready. My mom had gotten her some stuff to put in her hair, and now it floated around her face in delicate, caramel-colored tendrils.

Delicate, caramel-colored tendrils. I'm really starting to worry myself.

Anyway. We all got ready. We were wearing clean clothes. We went to school with various levels of enthusiasm.

The school was long and low and spread out, painted in dusty pastels so it coordinated with the desert. It was not fenced in. There was a ton of open space around it, plenty of places to take off from, land, escape from.

Jeb stood by the car, knowing better than to try to hug any of us good-bye. I was almost inside when he called my name.

"Max."

I went back over to him. "Please don't impart any pearls of wisdom. I just ate."

He shook his head. "Just—beware of Mr. Chu. He makes Itex look like Sesame Street."

Then, while I stared at him, he got in the car and drove away, headed for a plane to California. Which cheered me up but only a little.

We were met at the door of the school by a woman holding a clipboard. "Hello," she said, smiling. Her smile reached her eyes, an important trait. "I'm Ms. Hamilton, Max. It's good to finally meet you. Your mom and I went to college together. Welcome to the Day and Night School. I hope you'll be happy here." She paused, only momentarily taken aback at the sight of Total, trotting along by Angel's side.

Don't hold your breath, I thought. That's when it hit me: when had I last heard the Voice? I frowned, trying to remember. I couldn't. It was ages ago, or at least a week. A week can seem like a really long time in my life. Was I down to just one personality inside my head?

"First we need to test your knowledge, so we'll know your strengths and weaknesses," Ms. Hamilton went on cheerfully. "Then we'll know what classes will be best for you."

Nudge skipped along at Ms. Hamilton's side, glancing back to beam at me. I managed a slight grimace in return. We walked down a couple of hallways. There were exits at reassuring intervals. Through glass-paned doors, we saw large, sunny classrooms with small groups of kids in them. The kids looked happy to be here. Saps.

Ms. Hamilton took us to an empty classroom. We sat down in chairs that were designed to accommodate the wingless. I shot pained looks at everyone who met my eye, letting them know that this was not my idea of a good time.

I couldn't believe they had decided to do this. It was like—my plans for our lives weren't good enough anymore. They actually thought this situation would be better—which, I might add, included *not* being led by me.

Now my stomach hurt, and I felt weighed down by a gray cloud.

"First, we'll see how you do at math."

I tried not to groan out loud. We're street-smart, not book-smart. How many people had tested us over the years?

"Math, okay, bring it," said Total, hopping up on a chair. "Are we allowed to use calculators? Do you have some that are, you know, paw-ready?" He held up his right paw.

Ms. Hamilton stopped and stared at Total. I snickered to myself. I had *almost* forgotten how much fun it could be to bait people. I sat up a little straighter.

Then Ms. Hamilton smiled.

At Total.

"No, we don't have any paw-ready calculators," she said. "But you probably won't need one for these questions, anyway."

Just like that, this grown-up had accepted the talking dog.

Four hours later, Ms. Hamilton told us that our reading levels ranged between first grade and twelfth grade and that we had amazing vocabularies. (Angel was not the one who read on a first grade level, and Fang, Iggy, and I were not, sadly, the ones who read on a twelfth grade level.) We spelled about as well as four-year-olds do but had off-the-chart visual memories. We were majorly lame at math but could solve most problems anyway.

"In short, you're very, very, very bright kids who haven't had much schooling," said Ms. Hamilton.

I could have told her that before we'd wasted all this time. And she didn't even know about the other stuff we could do, like hack computers and jack cars and break into most buildings.

"Angel, you're so far off the chart that we'll have to invent a special chart just for you." Ms. Hamilton laughed.

"I thought you might," Angel said.

I'd been here five hours, and so far I hadn't really wanted to take anyone apart. Weird.

But that didn't mean I wanted to *stay* at the Day and Night School.

Was I the only one?

18

"SOUTH AMERICA," I said coaxingly. "It'll be warm. They have llamas. You like llamas."

Nudge crossed her arms over her chest. "I want to stay here."

We were in her room at a safe house that belonged to the school. It wasn't a bad setup. God knows we've had worse. But it was still part of a bigger confining situation, and my skin was crawling.

"How long do you think it will take another suicide sniper to find us?" I asked.

Nudge shrugged. "This place is out in the desert. And Ms. Hamilton told us about all the safety measures—the alarms, the lights, the radar. This is what we've been looking for."

A year ago I would have ignored what Nudge was

saying and just browbeaten her into getting up, throwing her stuff together, and bugging out.

And it would have worked. But we'd been through a lot in the past year. There had been a couple of times when the flock had almost split up. The stuff I had done to make sure we'd survive when the others were little was not the same stuff that would work now. I needed a new way to bend them to my will.

Only problem was, I didn't have any other way. And Nudge had found something she wanted even more—more than me, more than the flock, maybe even more than survival.

She wanted to learn.

"I'm tired of being scared, Max," she said, her large, coffee-colored eyes pleading.

"We all are! And as soon as we finish our big mission, we'll be able to relax. I promise!"

Note: I mentioned the Big Mission, the apocalypse, the end of the world, and so on. Basically, I'm supposed to "save the world." As in, save the entire freaking world. Jeb said everything that had happened to me, to us, was to toughen me up and teach me survival skills. In a way, everything seems like part of that plan, like it's connected. Like we have people trying to kill us *partly* because they think we're genetic mistakes, dangerous experiments that have gone wrong and so need to be eliminated—*and* partly because other people think that if I save the world, it'll cut way into their profit margins.

I have to believe that if I keep trying to figure out the bigger picture, it'll all make sense. If it doesn't, I'll be ready for a loony bin. And as hard as all that was for me to accept, it had to be even harder for the younger kids.

"I just want to fit in," Nudge said. She looked down at her tan feet, side by side on the new, clean carpet. "I want to be like other kids."

I breathed in to the count of four. "Nudge, most of the other kids here seem like spineless, gullible weenies who wouldn't survive one day on their own," I said gently.

"That's the point!" Nudge said. "They don't need to! They're not *on* their own—people take care of them."

"I've always taken care of you and the others as best I could," I said, stung.

Nudge's eyes softened. "But you're just a kid yourself." She brushed her fluffy hair behind one ear. "Max, I want to stay."

Time to get firm.

"We can't stay," I said briskly, standing up. "You know that. We have to go. This has been, well, not fun exactly but better than a punch in the gut. But it's over now, and we have to get back to reality, however much that might suck."

"I'm staying."

Had I heard her right? Nudge was always on my team. She was the agreeable one. Sure, she talked a whole lot and had a weird interest in clothes and fashion, but she was my... Nudge. Almost never in a bad mood. Never fought with the others.

"What?" I said, my mind reeling.

"I want to be normal. I want to be like other kids. I'm tired of being a freak and having to run all the time and never being able to settle down. I want a home. And I know how to get one."

My chest felt tight, but I forced myself to say, "How?"

Nudge mumbled something, her hair covering her face as she looked down.

"What?" I asked again.

"If I don't have wings."

This time I'd heard it, though it was barely a mumbled whisper.

"Nudge, you *come* with wings," I said, not even understanding what she meant. "You're the winged *version*. There's no *optional* Nudge with *no wings*."

She mumbled something again, which sounded bizarrely like, "Take them off." Then she was crying, and I sat back down and held her. Her tears got my shirt wet and her hair kept tickling my nose so I had to keep blowing little puffs of air to keep it away from my face. I was so horrified by what she'd said that it took a couple minutes to come up with something.

"Nudge, getting your wings taken off won't make you not a bird kid," I said. I am not at my best in situations like this and mostly just wanted to smack someone and say, "Snap out of it!" So I was really stretching here. "Being in the flock is more than just about having wings. You're different from other people all the way down to your bones and your blood cells."

She sobbed harder, and I backtracked quickly.

"What I mean is, you're special, every bit of you. More special than any other kid in the whole world, including the ones you want to be like. You're beautiful, and powerful, and unique. Kids without wings don't have your strength, your smarts, your determination. Remember that guy in the junkyard when we were stealing those bits of cable? Whose idea was it to hit him with a two-by-four, huh? Yours!"

Nudge sniffled.

"Remember when Gazzy was really starting to imitate things, all the time, and he kept sneaking up on us and making a police-siren sound, and we'd always freak? Who was it who taped his mouth shut with duct tape while he slept? You."

She nodded against my soggy shoulder.

"And what about that time we tried to shoplift underwear from Walmart, and the store manager was chasing us? You ripped a fire extinguisher right off the wall and hurled it at his feet, didn't you? He went down like a lead balloon, and we got away."

Nudge was silent. I was congratulating myself for averting disaster when she said quietly, "There's a difference between being special and being a total freak. I'm a total freak. And I'm staying here."

19

"THEN SHE SAID that she is a total freak and that she's staying here. After everything I came up with, everything I could think of, she said she's staying here."

My voice seemed unnaturally loud in the quiet night air, and I lowered it. Next to me, Fang leaned back against a huge boulder that was still warm from the day's sun. After my unsuccessful emo-weep-apalooza in Nudge's room, Fang and I had flown out into the desert, to a bare place where we could see anything coming from miles away.

Fang frowned and rubbed his forehead. "She's confused," he said. "She's just a kid."

"You know we have to go," I said. "What if she really won't come with us?"

The moon lit the contours of his face. His eyes were the same color as the sky—just as deep, just as dark.

"How can we force her?"

He'd said "we," which made me feel better. But the hard truth was that we couldn't force Nudge. "Even if we made her come," I admitted, "she'd just hold it against us. She'd be mad."

Fang nodded slowly. "You have to want to be with someone, or it doesn't work. You have to choose."

I searched his face, wondering if we were still talking about Nudge. "Uh, yeah," I said awkwardly. I was just about to say something really important about Nudge, and it flew right out of my mind. "Um, and she..." I tried, but my voice trailed off as I got lost in the intensity of Fang's expression.

He leaned closer. When had he gotten so much bigger than me? Four years ago he'd been a skinny beanpole! Now he was—

"I choose *you*," he said very softly, "*Max*."

Then his hard, rough hand tenderly cupped my chin, and suddenly his mouth was on mine, and every synapse in my brain shorted out.

We had kissed a couple of times before, but this was different. This time, I squelched my immediate, overwhelming desire to run away screaming. I closed my eyes and put my arms around him despite my fear. Then somehow we slid sideways so we were lying in the cool sand. I was holding him fiercely, and he was kissing me fiercely, and it was... just so, so intensely *good*. There aren't any words to describe how good it was. Once I got past my usual, gut-wrenching terror, there was a long, sweet slide into mindlessness, when all I felt was Fang, and all I heard was his breathing, and all I could think was, "Oh, God, I want to do this *all the time*."

Gradually our kisses became less hungry and more comforting. Our arms relaxed as we held each other in the cool desert air. Our breathing calmed, and my thoughts began to sort of connect to each other again in comprehensible chunks. I started my inevitable hysterical freak-out, but I tried to do it very quietly inside my head, because this had been so special, and I didn't want to ruin it. Like I usually did.

I slanted my gaze up to him, and Fang was... smiling. He was lying on his back, holding me against him, and he was looking up at the night sky, with the katrillion stars that you see only when you're in the middle of nowhere. Then you see stars that you never even knew existed. He was smiling, and his face looked softer and less closed.

I was instantly full of sharp, witty jibes, and it took every ounce of Maximum self-control not to say them. To just lie there and feel vulnerable, and think about everything that had just happened between us, and wonder how it had changed things, and wonder when I had started to love him so much, so painfully, and feel how terrified I was and how elated, and how every cell of my body felt so alive.

It was pretty much the worst thing that could ever happen to a girl.

I highly recommend it.

When Fang asked if it was time to get back, I thought hazily, *Back to what?*

This is my brain: O

This is my brain after making out with Fang: •

It's very sad.

Then a couple neurons fired in unison, and I remembered. *Oh, back to the entire rest of my family, including Nudge who wants to get her wings cut off.*

We hit the sky, and I flew powerfully, wincing only a little at the recently patched section. It was good, it was solid, but it needed a few more days.

"Whoa," said Fang, and I saw it too. I checked the stars—it was about 2 a.m.

Our newest safe house, alone in the desert, was ablaze with lights. Every window, every doorway.

Never a good sign.

20

IN AN INSTANT, all my warm fuzzies were replaced by stomach-churning fear and guilt. I hadn't been there. Something had happened, and I'd been locking lips with Fang out in the desert. How *stupid* could I get? This was exactly why I shouldn't do stuff like that!

We came down fast, hitting the ground hard in a running stop that kicked up dust. The front door flew open; Gazzy ran out.

I grabbed his arms. "What happened?"

"Max! Fang!" Gazzy yelled. He swallowed. "I thought you were gone! I thought they had gotten you!"

"No, no, sweetie. Just a little nighttime spin," I said quickly. "What's going on? Why's everyone up?"

Nudge and Iggy came out next—where was Angel? My

heart seized just as she appeared, with Total behind her. Thank God.

Suddenly it was quiet, the kind of quiet you have out in the desert in the middle of the night when everyone around you goes silent at the same time. Nudge, Iggy, Gazzy, Angel, and Total focused on me and Fang, their faces upset.

I looked from one to the next. They were really freaked, but they weren't trying to escape anything. They weren't bloody. They hadn't been in battle in the past twenty minutes.

"What. Is. Going. On?" I asked very deliberately, searching their eyes.

"It's, uh..." Nudge began, then cleared her throat. She glanced at the others, then tried again, meeting my gaze bravely. "It's your mom, Max. Dr. Martinez. She's been kidnapped. She's gone."

21

I'M THE FLOCK LEADER. I'm fast, I'm tough, and I can think on my feet or in flight. My hair-trigger responses have saved our hides more times than I can count. So my brain kicked in to high gear right away as I cut to the heart of the matter.

"Huh?" I managed. I felt like I'd just taken a karate chop to the chest.

"Phone call," Iggy said.

"Ella called," Nudge clarified. "She's hysterical—your mom disappeared from the airport this afternoon while they were between flights. Dr. Martinez just went to the restroom and never came back. Right now Ella's at her aunt's house. I don't think Jeb knows. Ella was going to call him after she talked to us." She took a deep breath. For once I didn't mind her wordiness—the more info I had, the better.

"Did they call the police or the FBI?" I asked, already calculating how long it would take me to fly to my half sister.

"We don't know," Nudge said. Then we heard the phone ringing inside. I raced in and grabbed it.

"Max?" It was Dr. John Abate, one of my mom's colleagues at the CSM. "Max, are you all okay?"

"Yes," I said tensely. I motioned to the others to get inside and lock the door, turn off the lights. We could be the next targets. "What's going on?" I punched the button to put him on speakerphone.

"A fax just came in to the CSM office," Dr. Abate said. "Usually no one would be here at this hour, but a couple of us were putting together a press report. Anyway—this fax came, and it says that Valencia has been kidnapped."

"Yeah, Ella called." I was pacing, trying not to bite my nails. "Who was the fax from?"

"We don't know," said Dr. Abate. "It looks like the origination number got cut off somehow during transmission. But it says that Valencia has been kidnapped and will be held until the CSM quits its efforts to put pressure on big businesses."

My head whirled. I remembered Mr. Chu telling me that he'd come up with a way to convince me to quit working with the CSM. Maybe he'd just found it.

"Uh-huh," I said. "Anything else?"

"Yes," John said. "Just a minute ago, we received another fax. It showed Valencia being held hostage. She was alive when the picture was taken, but we don't know how long ago that was. We enlarged the photo, and the weird thing is, the background looks like she's being held on a boat."

"Boat?" That didn't add up to anything. Oh, *wait*. Yes it did. When Mr. Chu's M-Geeks had grabbed me, they'd taken me to a boat. I remembered the rocking sensation. Crap.

"We've called the FBI, of course," said John. "They're going over everything now. Someone's flying to Arizona to meet with Ella, see if she remembers anything helpful. But I wanted to make sure you guys were okay."

"Yeah, we're okay." If "okay" was broadened to include the feeling of having your heart ripped out and stomped on.

Life was easier when it was just the six of us. I'd had five other bird kids to worry about, protect, keep in line, care about. Now I had Total—who had somehow glommed on to us, I don't even know how—and my mom, and my half sister. My circle was still expanding, and it was too hard for me to keep track of everyone, keep everyone safe. I'd certainly failed here. Not telling anyone about Mr. Chu and his threats had put my mom in danger. Maybe cost her her life.

"Max, you there?" Dr. Abate asked.

"Yes." One-word answers seemed all I was capable of.

"Listen—I've got to go talk to the FBI. They'll probably want to talk to you too. You were among the last people to see her. I want you guys to sit tight for a couple hours, okay?"

"Hm," I said, unwilling to promise that.

"Hole up there, protect yourselves, but stay put," he said again. "Let me get some answers before you go charging off."

"I do not 'go charging off!'" I said, offended.

"Yes, you do," John said, exactly when everyone else in the flock said it.

"Your *middle name* is 'Charging Off,'" Total muttered, fortunately out of kicking range.

"Okay, gotta go," said John. "We're going to try to figure out if we can tell where the boat was by what we can see in the picture. I'll call you as soon as I can. Stay by the phone."

"Okay." I hung up, just as Fang turned toward me from the window.

"In other news," he said, "the house is surrounded. It looks like those things from Mexico City."

22

SITTING TIGHT? Holing up? Waiting for answers?

Those are all things *I'm not good at*.

Planning a massive attack against mechanical geeky-like things when I was already furious and itching to kill something?

Piece o' cake.

I took a break from my plotting, clenching and unclenching my hands, to find five pairs of eyes locked on to mine. Iggy's gaze was locked to a point about two inches above my eyebrows. He's good, but he's not perfect.

"What?" I said.

"Dr. Abate said to sit tight," Nudge said.

"Dr. Abate didn't know about the combat robots sent to kill us," I pointed out.

"They haven't attacked yet," Iggy said.

"Oh, gosh, I guess they *won't,* then," I said, rolling my eyes. "I just rolled my eyes, Ig. Anyway, how many of them are there?"

"Looks like, about . . . eighty." Fang calculated the odds in his head. He nodded once: we could do it.

I began to come up with an attack plan.

"Maximum Ride."

My eyebrows raised. The voice from outside had been loud, mechanical, and had mispronounced my name. Max-HIH-mum Ride. What a doofus.

Gazzy had been kneeling at a window, curtain raised just enough for him to see. "These guys have . . . it looks like Uzis attached to their arms. Uzis. The automatic ones."

He glanced at me, willing me to understand that it wouldn't be hand-to-wing combat. Eighty-plus submachine guns spewing countless rounds of bird-kid-piercing bullets would be significantly less fun than the rip-roarin', head-breakin', ankle-bustin' jamboree I'd pictured.

"Hm," I said.

"Max-HIH-mum Ride," the voice intoned again.

I let out a deep breath. "Everyone, get upstairs to the hall, where there aren't any windows. Stay down, but be ready to do an up-and-away if you hear a bunch of breaking glass." I looked at Fang. Our hot-and-heavy make-out session in the desert seemed like a lifetime ago. Two lifetimes. "Should I answer him?" I asked, only half joking.

"I think you should look at him," Fang said, and something in his voice made me frown.

As the flock scuttled upstairs, I sank to my knees and crawled to a window. Despite Gazzy's repeated pleas that we get a pair of night-vision goggles, we do see excellently in the dark. So it wasn't hard for me to focus on the leader in front, the one calling my name.

What I saw was like ice water being poured down my back.

I looked at Fang, who was crouched in the living room's darkness, waiting.

"But he's . . . dead," I said, my voice hollow. "I mean, dead *again*."

Fang's face was grim. "They just made it look like that to freak you out."

I nodded slowly. "They succeeded."

The head robot-soldier had been enhanced, its outer covering made to look more human. Made to look exactly like Ari, my half brother, who I'd killed once, saw killed once, and had buried not that long ago.

23

MY FIRST THOUGHT was *Jeb*. He'd created the first Ari—maybe he'd had enough DNA left to create another one. Then I thought about how distraught Jeb had seemed at Ari's funeral.

I took another look.

There were slight differences. The curve of his eyebrows, the wave of his hair. Maybe it wasn't really Ari's genes. Just a similar thing made to freak me out, like Fang said.

"So where are these guys from?" Fang asked quietly, crouching next to me on the floor. "They were in Mexico City. Now they're here. What do they want?"

"They want me—us—to quit working for the CSM," I said. "Remember when I came back with my new, ventilated wing? They did it—they took me to a guy called Mr. Chu. Short, I think he's Chinese, major bee up his butt. Mr. Chu told me he'd find a way to make me stop working for the CSM. He said he represented a bunch of super-powerful businessmen."

"And your response was..."

"Unsatisfactory, I guess." I peeped through the window again: The things had moved closer. They were about twenty yards from the house. The leader was still out front, and I sensed he was about to mispronounce my name again.

"And you didn't tell anyone because..." Fang had that too-patient tone in his voice that let me know that he knew that I knew that he knew that I'd screwed up.

"I wanted to do some research," I said too defensively, which let him know that I knew that he knew that I may have conceivably perhaps not chosen the best possible route in this particular instance. "Later I mentioned it to the Jebster, and he went pale like someone had sucked all the blood out of his head." Okay, I guess that's a gross image. But still. "And then he convincingly said, 'Gee, no, haven't heard of him.' As if I'd had my brain removed and I might believe that."

Fang said nothing, which meant that he was thinking. He says nothing and thinks more than anyone I know.

"Max-HIH-mum Ride," said the Ari wannabe.

"How hard would it be to program him to say my name correctly?" I fumed.

"You must not leave the area," said the voice.

I peeked out through the curtain again. The Ari-thing was closer, standing directly in the moonlight. I peered at him, and something about him made my blood run cold—and it wasn't just his Ari-ness.

"Fang," I whispered. "Look at him. He might not be a robot."

Fang rose slightly and took a look. "Hm." There was a whole unspoken paragraph there. You had to read between the lines.

I looked out again. The combat-bots were huddled together, forming an almost perfect circle that I assumed went around the whole house. Their knees were bent, their Uzi-arms raised and braced. Primed and ready for action.

But it was the main guy who stuck out. Despite his jerky movements and mechanical voice, he seemed oddly—human.

"Ew," I whispered, struck by a thought. "You know how Itex stretched skin stuff over their 'bots to make 'em look like Erasers, or just more humanoid? This guy—it's like they took a person and then built a robot *inside* of him. Going from the inside out instead of the outside in. You know? Gross." My nose wrinkled as I pondered this.

Fang looked at me silently for a few seconds. "Is it hard, being you?"

"Yes, it *is,* actually," I said snidely. "For the record. But are you saying that that's *impossible?* That no one could *possibly* be twisted enough to take a person and then grow a *cyborg* inside it? Gosh, *that* couldn't happen, not in today's world!" I made my eyes big. "That's almost as unbelievable as a bunch of scientists grafting *avian DNA* into human embryos! It's the stuff of science fiction! It couldn't possibly *ever* happen!"

"Why are you shouting?" came Gazzy's whispered voice from the stairs.

"I'm *not* shouting!" I said, lowering my voice. "Just scoping out the enemy, as usual."

"Oh," said Gazzy. "Well, keep scoping, 'cause they're about to blow up."

24

YOU COULD LOCK the Gasman in a padded cell with some dental floss and a bowl of Jell-O, and he'd find a way to make something explode.

I immediately crawled away from the window and hunkered down behind the couch. "Blow up?" I repeated. With Gazzy, we take life-saving precautions first and ask questions later.

"If you leave the area, you will be terminated with extreme prejudice," said the voice outside.

Gazzy cackled. "What a butthead. Wait till you see what's gonna happen!"

I glanced at Fang, who had moved under a table. "Did you leave the flamethrowers lying around again?"

He shrugged. "I always forget."

Inside, the house suddenly seemed darker. I looked at the windows. There was no moonlight shining under the curtains. Then I heard the far-off rumble of thunder. We were in the middle of the desert—not a big rainstorm area.

"God in heaven. He can't manipulate the weather now, can he?" I asked Fang anxiously.

Fang dropped his head into his hands and groaned.

"Max-HIH-mum Ride."

"I AM a dumb-bot!" I couldn't help snickering. Fang's shoulders hunched.

More rumbling thunder. Windowpanes rattling. I peeped over the top of the couch and could barely see the leader-guy through the inch of exposed window. He was looking up at the sky with Ari's confused expression.

"Okay, here it comes," I heard Gazzy say from upstairs.

"Did you set the thing?" Iggy asked him.

"Yup."

"Point it away from the house?"

Oh, yes, please, point whatever it is away from the house, I wished fervently.

"Duh, yeah," said Gazzy. He chuckled. "Should be any second."

Suddenly the entire area was lit with a massive lightning bolt—despite the curtains and shades on the windows, the living room was as bright as day. At almost the exact same time, there was a horrible buzzing, crackling sound, and every bit of electricity in the house died—tiny status lights winking out, the AC halting abruptly. Then there was a huge boom of thunder that I felt deep in my stomach.

With an ear-throbbing *pop!* it was over.

Silence.

"Oh, way, *way* awesome, dude!" Gazzy shouted, laughing maniacally. I heard many slappings of high fives.

"Did it do it?" Iggy asked. "Never mind—I can smell it."

"It *so* did it, man!" Gazzy said excitedly. "This was the *pinnacle* of our pyromania!" I stood up cautiously as he raced downstairs. Fang crawled out from under the table.

"Max!" Gazzy said, running to me. "We saw big thunderheads forming in the distance—the first time in years, I bet! Then—check it out! This house had a lightning rod on the roof! That's a metal pole that sends any lightning bolts into the ground. We disconnected it, aimed it at the dumb-bots, and enhanced its powers a tad! Next thing you know, they're extracrispy! And the best part? They were standing so close together that they helped fry each other!" He hugged himself, jumping up and down. "I'm brilliant! I'm a genius! I can blow up the world!"

I raised my eyebrows.

"Not that I would *want* to, of course," Gazzy said, and gave a little cough.

"Should we look outside?" Total asked.

Fang was already standing at a window, using one finger to move a curtain aside. "They're fried, all right. There's barely enough parts left to make a can opener."

Gazzy and Iggy crowed some more and slapped high fives again. Somehow, even though he can't see, Iggy never misses a high five. It's a little creepy.

I opened the front door slowly. There was a wide, charred circle around the house, littered with 'bot bits and smoking electronics. "See if there are any salvageable weapons," I directed. The Ari ~~dobblyganga~~ ~~doppergung~~ ~~dobblemunger~~ look-alike was lying on the ground, mostly in one piece. Mostly human, with a 'bot substructure. Again, ew.

I walked over to him, and it was pretty awful. I can destroy a hundred 'bots and still whistle cheerfully, but this poor mess on the ground seemed as much a victim as we were. Some crucial parts of him were missing, but his eyes blinked as I approached. This close, he still looked a ton like Ari, but I could tell it wasn't a perfect copy.

Then I remembered that this creature had been prepared to exterminate my *family,* and that my own *mother* had been *kidnapped,* and that the flock had been hiding in the dark wondering if they were about to *die.*

"So," I said, leaning down a bit, "how's Mr. Chu, that scamp?"

His head twitched, and the light behind his eyes went out.

"Tell him hi for me!" I said, then looked at the flock. "Pack light. We're moving out."

25

THE PHONE RANG just as we reentered the dark house. I stared at it.

"Regular corded phone. Not connected to the electrical system," Iggy clarified, somehow knowing what we were all wondering.

I grabbed it. "What?"

"Max—good, you're there," said John Abate. "We've got some details about Valencia's disappearance, but I don't want to discuss them on the phone. We've been tipped that your house might be under surveillance."

"Um, not so much," I said, thinking of the mess outside.

"To be on the safe side, we're sending a car for you. It should be there in about an hour."

"It'll be dawn then," I said, suddenly feeling exhausted and headachy and newly upset about my mom. "Better make it an armored one."

26

THE SIGHT OF DAWN breaking over the horizon, slowly dispelling the darkness with tendrils of pink and cream, literally the start of a brand-new day—you know how that fills people with joy and hope and a will to somehow go on?

Those people are nuts.

Our dawn showcased a football field of destruction: charred earth, shattered cacti, a blackened spew of twisted metal and melted wires, plus the mangled wreck of some poor sap who had been created to be a weapon in someone else's war.

We were all waiting in the living room when the armored Hummer arrived in a cloud of dust. Angel and Gazzy were asleep. Nudge was sitting, unusually quiet, her chin resting in her hands. Iggy and Total were snoring on the other couch.

I was purposely not looking at Fang. After making some progress, so to speak, with whatever was happening between us, I felt all my protective shields firmly locked in place again. I couldn't believe how vulnerable I'd allowed myself to be. It had been a mistake.

Fang was going to kill me when I told him. Yeah, I was looking forward to that.

When the car arrived, I checked it out from behind a curtain. Dr. John Abate stepped out of it, looking anxiously at the evidence of the fight. I opened the front door of the house.

"Hi," I said. I'd met him several times, and he seemed okay. I knew he was one of my mom's best friends, and his face showed the worry he was feeling.

His face relaxed, and he came over. "They got the worst of it, huh?" he asked, gesturing to the piles of remains.

"Always do," I said tiredly.

"Max!"

I froze at the new voice. Yes. To make my evening of horror complete, Dr. Brigid Dwyer stepped out of the Hummer and hurried over to me with a big smile, her red hair flashing.

I allowed myself to be hugged.

"I'm so, so sorry about your mom," she said sincerely. "We'll get her back—I promise."

I nodded, then stood there like a dummy as the rest of

the flock came out of the house to be hugged by Brigid. Watching her hug Fang, seeing his arms go around her, was almost enough to make me hurl.

I might need to rethink my protective armor a bit.

"Let's hurry," said Dr. Abate. "We've got a plane waiting. On the way, you can fill me in on what happened. And vice versa."

"Max," said Nudge, and instinctively I braced. I'd known something was up.

"Get in the car, sweetie," I said, pretending not to notice anything was wrong.

She swallowed. "I'm staying."

"You can't. It's not safe."

"I'll be safe at the school, in the dorms," she said. She gestured limply to the house, its surrounding wreckage. "I can't do this anymore. I want to go to school. I just want to be a kid. At least for a while."

I had a million excellent arguments why she was wrong and making the biggest mistake of her life, and I opened my mouth to get started, and then it hit me: it would be pointless. Nudge wasn't four or five. She was around eleven and would be as tall as me in another year or so. She really meant she *couldn't do this anymore.*

If she didn't want to be with us, didn't want to fight, she would get hurt—bad. She might cause one of us to get hurt or killed. I needed my flock to be fierce, bloodthirsty warriors. Nudge's heart just wasn't in it, and *I couldn't fix that*. Oh, God.

I swallowed hard, making my chin stiff, my mouth firm. I'm the flock leader because *I can do* the gnarly jobs. "You may *not* get your wings taken off," I said sternly.

Wonder dawned in her big brown eyes as she realized what I was saying. A huge smile lit her face, and she hugged me fiercely, forcing the air from my lungs. "You may get your ears pierced," I croaked, trying to breathe. "Or your nose. Or—actually, nothing else. And you absolutely, positively, may never, *ever* get your wings removed, or I swear to God, I will come kick your skinny, fashion-conscious butt into next week. Do you hear me?"

"Yes!" Nudge said happily. "Yes, yes! Thank you, thank you, thank you! I love you *so* much!"

Ever notice how often people say that right before they say good-bye?

Part Two

WE ALL LIVE IN A DEADLY SUBMARINE

27

THE ARMORED CAR drove for about an hour through the desert, ending up at a military airfield. Nothing like passing through heavy, barbed-wire-topped gates to make a girl feel secure! And by *secure,* I mean supertwitchy. At least we could fly out of here if we needed to. I eyed the antiaircraft guns mounted on turrets and hoped they'd be considered overkill for bird kids.

Despite the fact that we were really tired, really hungry, and really upset about my mom, we did manage to fill John and Brigid in on everything that had happened. John showed me the two faxes they'd gotten. Seeing my mom looking straight ahead, fear in her eyes as some goon held a gun on her, made my blood boil.

I was going to track down the kidnappers if it meant flying to every single boat in the entire world.

"We're taking a military jet to San Diego," said John. "The FBI is meeting us at the navy base there. We'll go over all the information we have, and see what we can get out of it."

I nodded numbly, looking at the soldiers bustling about, each one having somewhere to be. I wondered if Nudge was back at the school yet. I guessed she was.

The armored car drove right up to a small jet, its stairs already pulled down.

"Please tell me there's food on board," said Iggy.

"Yes," said John. "A whole lot of it. I was warned about how much you guys ate on the *Wendy K*." His tired smile made me think back to our days of living on that boat with Brigid and the other scientists.

I glanced over at Brigid as she talked quietly to Fang, and my stomach knotted. He was paying attention to her but also looking at me pretty often. The whole thing was complicated and messy, and I hated it.

But I loved him. And I guess the messiness went along with that.

"It'll be okay, Max," Angel whispered, patting my hand.

I looked at her, wondering if she was talking about my mom or Nudge or Fang.

"Everything," she said softly. "Everything will be okay."

I managed a tight smile, and then we were all climbing out of the Hummer and walking across hot tarmac to the jet.

A quick, happy bark made my head snap up. There, at the top of the jet stairs, was Akila!

"Oh. My. God," Total breathed, stopping dead. He stared up at her as if he were a starving man and she was a Snickers bar. He shook his head. "I know it's daylight, because the sun has started to shine again!" He inhaled deeply. "And the air—the air is suddenly perfumed with—"

"Jet fuel, hot tar, dirty bird kids, and a Malamute," I said, nudging him forward with my foot. "Just get on the plane." Not everything has to be a Broadway show, you know?

Total shot me an aggrieved glance as he trotted up the jet's stairs. At the top, he and Akila happily licked each other's faces, their tails wagging. It was—well, actually, I hate to admit—it was kind of sweet. In a slobbery kind of way.

We were all waiting for Total and Akila to move inside when Total stepped back and, with a flourish, opened his small black wings. Akila blinked. And if a Malamute can look surprised, she looked it.

"Regard, my princess!" said Total, fluttering his wings. "At last, I might be worthy of your beauty!" He knelt before her and kissed one of her front paws. She licked the top of his head. I glanced around, and everyone was grinning.

Oh yeah. Love is great, just great.

28

THE MAN IN THE CRISP WHITES saw us as soon as he came in the door. We were in some building smack-dab in the middle of the biggest naval base on the West Coast. Frankly, I'd rather be at the San Diego Zoo, but at least this place was air-conditioned.

We were in a conference room, ready to meet with some grown-ups, and I was thinking that I had already played in this scenario more times than I could count. Who remembers *any* of those situations ending well? Go on, raise your hand. No one?

Right.

However, using insidious and irresistible mind-control techniques such as offering us Mountain Dew and a ton of nachos, the naval bigwigs had managed to corral us in this room for a debriefing.

Unfortunately, every time someone said "debriefing," the entire flock had one image: someone's tighty-whities disappearing in a flash. We were smothering our giggles, but it was getting harder. Coupled with the whole "naval this, and naval that," with its undeniable belly-button connotations, we were essentially turning into a sugar-jacked, sleep-deprived flock of incoherent, silly, recombinant-DNA goofballs. This was not going to end well.

This guy had come in, and everyone turned to him as if now the party could get started. Tucking a sheaf of papers under one arm, he frowned and looked at the woman in the blazer with all the stars on the shoulders. We'd met her. She was Admiral Bellows. (I am not making this up.)

"Why are these children here?" he asked brusquely.

"Thank you for joining us, Commander," said Admiral Bellows. She had short, tidy gray hair and seemed extremely no-nonsense. "These children are integral to our investigation. For one thing, this child, Max, is Dr. Martinez's daughter."

Huh. She'd called me a child, not a mutant freak. And I was a daughter, not just the result of one of Dr. Martinez's eggs being fertilized in a test tube. It felt weirdly—normal.

"All the more reason this conference is inappropriate for children," the commander said pointedly.

"We're very sensitive, you know," said Iggy.

The admiral shot Iggy a sharp glance, which of course was wasted on him. "These children are different," she told the commander. "Please come in and share your findings, Commander. Time is of the essence."

I decided I kind of liked her.

The commander paused as if trying to think of a new way to win the argument but was distracted when Total put both front paws on the conference table.

"Excuse me," he said, using one paw to brush a nacho crumb from his muzzle. "You think you could scrounge up some pico de gallo? Maybe even some guac? And how about a nice cold Evian for my lady friend here?" He gestured to where Akila was sitting with quiet dignity by Dr. Abate.

The flock managed to remain straight-faced.

"It's okay, Commander," I said in the deafening silence. "Like the admiral said, we're different." I shrugged out of my hoodie and extended my wings, all thirteen feet of brown glory. They are stunning, I must say. Even with the still-slightly-visible boo-boo on one.

Everyone in the room except John and Brigid were mesmerized. The commander's mouth actually dropped open a bit, and I ruffled my primary feathers a little. "So how 'bout we just get on with the show, eh? We're talking about my mom here."

Between the talking dog and the girl with wings, the

commander was pretty much a squashed bug. Wordlessly he gave a DVD to a navy guy working the computer, and the lights were dimmed. A PowerPoint presentation began on the white wall opposite the table.

The first slide said: THE BIRDS ARE WORKING.

29

"THE BIRDS ARE WORKING." What the heck did that mean? And what did it have to do with my mom? As you know, I've been kidnapped myself, and let me tell you, "total bummer" doesn't begin to describe it. The thought of my mom going through what I had gone through was making me nuts.

The slide was followed by a grainy movie.

"This was filmed yesterday evening at nineteen hundred hours, at twenty-one degrees, thirty minutes north; one hundred fifty-seven degrees, forty minutes west," said Commander Crisp Pants.

"In the Pacific Ocean, off the coast of Hawaii," the admiral clarified for us civilians.

The movie started off with an aerial view, like from a plane, then focused lower and lower over the water. Lots of fuzzy action tightened up to reveal... major bird-o-rama. Hundreds, no, *thousands* of seabirds. Gulls, albatrosses, cormorants, and a bunch I didn't recognize. They hovered just a few feet above the water, covering it thickly, and they seemed to be—feeding or attacking in a frenzy or I had no idea what.

"It's like, free-shrimp day or something!" Gazzy said, awed.

"What are they doing?" I asked, impatient to get to the part about my mom.

"We don't know. But wait," said Commander Crisp Pants. The camera pulled back to reveal a small fishing boat, maybe a couple hundred yards away from the bird frenzy. We could see the crew, all watching the birds from on deck, gesturing and looking amazed. Some looked scared. I read the name on the side: *Nani Moku*.

All of a sudden, something from beneath the water smashed up through the fishing boat, capsizing it. The boat was literally broken in half. The crew flailed about in the water, trying to cling to debris. What was left of the boat sank within moments. We saw some of the fishermen trying to save their comrades, saw one guy realize his friend was dead in the water.

"Was that a whale, Commander?" the admiral asked.

"Unknown. It could have been a whale or a submarine. We've gone over this footage a hundred times with no success. But now, look at this."

The film ended, and a greenish, dim, very grainy picture flashed up on the screen. I almost yelled: it was my mom.

She was looking straight ahead, her brown eyes scared but defiant. It looked like her arms were tied behind her back. Next to her, someone wearing a ski mask held up a *New York Times* to show yesterday's date. I'd love to know how they got their hands on that.

My stomach tightened. Fang's knee bumped mine under the table, the equivalent of a reassuring hug. Normally that would be all I needed to chill. But right then it hit me: this was not "normally." Nudge was gone. I hadn't even realized how much I depended on her sympathy in tough times.

"The camera focused tightly on Dr. Martinez, as you can see," said Commander Crisp Pants. "You can hardly make out any background. Except—" He nodded to the technician, and the picture zoomed in until it was hardly recognizable. The big white blob in one corner was part of my mom's elbow. The commander moved a red laser pointer over the blurred picture. "Except here. To us, this looks like a window frame." He moved over an unrecognizable lightish thing. "Or, more accurately, a porthole. And now look back here."

He moved the laser pointer, and I saw Total's head whipping back and forth. I made a mental note to never let Gazzy or Iggy get hold of a laser pointer.

Through the thick, wavy porthole glass, there was another jellylike blob. The commander ran his laser along a slightly darker blob. "Please enhance the sharpness by three hundred percent," he told the technician.

The next second, the conference room went still and silent. Though still way blurry, we could now make out that the darker blobs on the lighter blob through the blobby window were words. They were words on a piece of wood: *Nani Moku*.

The commander stood up, and the room lights were turned on. "We believe this picture was taken on a submarine," he announced. "We think the submarine was in the area, and probably capsized that boat, though we're not certain. But that's a piece of wreckage from that fishing boat, and it's under water. So they must be holding Dr. Martinez under water. And since we know that boat was capsized in the Pacific Ocean, off the coast of Hawaii, we believe that Dr. Martinez is somewhere around there."

I was ready to leap up and fly to Hawaii. From San Diego, it would take me about six or seven hours, I figured.

"What does 'The birds are working' mean?" the admiral asked.

The commander looked at her. "Again, unknown. But there was an audio clip with the bird film, and when we sped up the sound by five hundred percent, that was the phrase we heard."

"Max, sit down," said John Abate quietly.

I looked at him, halfway out of my chair.

"We have a plan," he went on. "We need your help. And that plan does not involve you charging off on your own."

"I do not charge off!" I insisted yet again.

"Maximum 'Charging Off' Ride," Total muttered under his breath.

I gritted my teeth and slowly sat back down. "You have one minute to tell me your plan. Make it good."

30

HERE ARE ALL the flies in my ointment:

1) The phrase "fly in the ointment." Like, yuck. Who came up with that?
2) We were on a private jet loaned to us by our old pal Nino Pierpont, aka the richest guy in the world. Technically, I was *being flown* to Hawaii.
3) I was not busting heads, taking names, or shaking anyone down for information.
4) Dr. Stupendous was still with us and still had red hair.
5) Nudge was still gone.
6) My mom was still kidnapped.
7) Fang was still Fang.

Dr. John Abate sat down next to where I was reclined in the schmancy leather chair, unsuccessfully trying to sleep. Not too long ago, I was bunking down on a concrete ledge in an abandoned subway tunnel. Now, here I was on a private jet, in the lap of luxury, covered by a cozy mohair throw...and, basically, I felt like my life sucked pretty much the same as always.

The main difference being that when I was on the concrete ledge, I actually got some sleep. And my whole flock was together. And I didn't even have a mom. Much less one I cared about. Much less one I cared about and who then got kidnapped, introducing countless new opportunities for pain.

I opened one eye. "Are we planning to dive-bomb the submarine? Is this plane equipped with marine missiles?"

John smiled weakly. "No. It's taking us to another U.S. Navy base, in Hawaii. The navy has agreed to help us get Valencia back."

"Has the CSM agreed to back off big companies?" I asked. Which might make Mr. Chu release my mom, as he promised.

John looked troubled. "No. We've been in discussions ever since we learned of Valencia's disappearance. We feel that Valencia would never forgive us if she found out they had made us cave. Especially over her. She's one of the founding members of the CSM and one of its most ardent supporters. To have it be dissolved over this—I just think she would hate it."

I thought for a minute. "You're probably right," I finally said, reluctantly.

"John?" Gazzy had his face pressed against a window.

"Yes?"

"What would happen if a big bird, like a goose, flew into the jet engine?"

Leave it to Gazzy.

"It would probably be very bad," said John.

"What would happen if someone hummed a football into the engine, right when the plane was taking off?" Gazzy looked thoughtful.

"Is there a point to this line of questioning?" John asked, rubbing his eyes.

"Just wondering," Gazzy said, his blue eyes innocent.

"I never thought I'd say this, but I actually miss Nudge's run-on mouth," said Iggy, completely changing the topic.

"I miss her smile," said Angel, looking up for a minute from where she was playing cards with Brigid. Brigid, thankfully, was smart enough not to play poker with Angel anymore.

"I miss her brownness," said Iggy, gazing sightlessly out the window.

"I'm sure she's fine," I said brusquely, trying to ignore the ache in my heart. "She made her choice."

"I miss her laugh," said Gazzy. "And, like, her, I don't know, girliness."

Yeah, we all know how lacking I am in that department. Compared to Nudge, I'm completely hopeless. And compared to Brigid, I'm—one of those body bags in boxing or something.

Just then Fang came over and sat next to me. John smiled at him and got up to go sit with Brigid and Angel.

Fang reclined his seat. After giving the cabin a casual glance, he slipped his hand under my blanket, finding my hand and holding it. I felt my cheeks reddening and hoped no one would notice.

"This sucks, about your mom," he said, his voice so low only I could hear it. I nodded, feeling the strength in his hand, the muscles and tendons, the bones, the calluses and scars. "And Nudge," he went on. I nodded again, mutely remembering that night out in the desert with Fang and then coming home to find disaster and chaos. And the next morning, Nudge leaving the flock. Suddenly my throat felt tight, and my eyelids were heavy. I closed them.

"I'm here." His voice was so soft, I wasn't even sure I'd heard it. But I had.

And there, with nine words, Fang had summed up everything I was thinking, everything I was feeling, everything in my past and my future.

He's your soulmate.

My eyes shot open. Voice? Are you back?

31

"WE THINK IT will take at least seven days, possibly more." The woman in the tailored khaki uniform looked at us impassively.

"No," I said, crossing my arms over my chest, just as Brigid said, "We don't have that much time."

"Then they can't come," said the woman in khaki.

Okay, first impressions of Hawaii? We'd arrived at sunset, and it had looked like a movie set, with fake molded plastic islands set into impossibly beautiful blue water. It reminded me of Fang's desire for us to find a deserted island somewhere and just live, peacefully, by ourselves. No world-saving. No 'bot-fighting. Just us, the sand, and the sea.

Our jet had landed at the naval base at Pearl Harbor, and we were immediately greeted by soft, gentle breezes, unusual floral scents, palm trees with actual coconuts on them, and this pit bull of a woman who was about to make me go seriously ballistic.

John and Brigid looked at me.

"I'm going, no matter what they say," I said in the steely voice I usually reserved for extreme circumstances, like when Gazzy had left crayons in his pocket during a rare instance of my running laundry through a dryer. We'd looked like flower children for months.

But the khaki woman wasn't in the armed forces for nothing. She met my eyes, and I had to admit, we were almost evenly matched in the freeze-out glare category. Now if I could just run her down with a tank, my day would perk right up.

"You cannot board a vessel of the United States Navy unless you satisfactorily pass a BSSTC, a basic survival skills training course," Lieutenant Khaki almost snarled. "This course normally takes three weeks. Under these extraordinary circumstances, we can compact it into one week. In the extremely unlikely event that you last a week, you may then board a United States Naval vessel in an attempt to ascertain Dr. Martinez's whereabouts, and, if possible, execute a rescue mission, under the supervision, direction, and authority of the United States Navy."

"You sure do like saying 'United States Navy,'" said Gazzy cheerfully.

Her gray eyes flared as she looked down at him.

"Lieutenant, I'm sure you can appreciate the very dire

need we have to begin the search as quickly as possible," John said firmly. "Admiral Bellows assured us that we would have every resource necessary."

"And so you shall," said Lieutenant Khaki, turning to him. "As soon as you pass a BS—"

"Yeah, we got the BS part," I interrupted. "But look, we have all the survival skills we need—and then some. You guys just don't have that much to teach us."

For a moment Lieutenant Khaki looked like she was about to laugh in amazement. Instead, she just snorted and motioned to a khaki-clad underling. "Ensign, please show our visitors—and their dogs—to their quarters."

"Yes, ma'am," said the young ensign, touching his cap.

As Total huffed indignantly, I whirled to stare at John. He looked upset and also tired and frustrated. I remembered that he cared about my mom too. He waved us closer.

"Guys," he said, "I'll make some phone calls, see what I can do. In the meantime, just do what they say. If they do agree to help us, it could mean the difference between life and death."

My mom's life or death.

"We need their resources," John went on. "And frankly, I don't know that we have any contacts with enough leverage to make the navy forgo their standard operating procedure. But, like I said, let me make some calls."

Reason and emotion battled inside my head. Where was my Voice when I actually needed it? I thought it had popped up earlier, but I wasn't sure if that had really been my Voice returning, or if Angel had been putting thoughts into my head. Or was it my own wishful thinking, blurting out something in the (somewhat relative, in my case) privacy of my mind?

At any rate, no Voice stepped up now to help me make a decision.

I hated this. Hated it. I'd always gotten us out of scrapes on my own. I'd never once had to agree to let some official person help us. But this was different. I knew I couldn't find my mom by myself or with just the flock. The Pacific Ocean is too big, too deep.

The fact that accepting this bitter reality practically made my psyche split in two is indicative of my trademark inability to work or play well with others. I missed the good old days, when I was just supposed to save the world. That was so much easier to stomach than having to save my mom.

After a minute, I nodded tensely. "They have to take us as soon as we pass the course," I snapped at John. "Even if it's less than a week."

He nodded. My jaw tight, chest aching, I turned to follow the ensign, who was waiting for us.

"Is there a mess hall?" Gazzy asked him. "Can we see your weapons? Can I drive a tank? Do you have a lot of explosives?"

The ensign looked besieged. "Yes, mess hall. No to the weapons. Major no to the tank. The explosives are nothing you'll get close to. Okay, kid?"

Gazzy looked disappointed.

Welcome to the khaki wonderland.

32

GIVEN OUR BACKGROUND, you need to know that having our lives take huge, bizarre nightmarish turns for the worse is kind of a regular thing. And yet when the alarm went off at five a.m. the next morning, I felt like we were exploring a whole new level of bad.

We had spent the night in an overturned metal halfpipe. John said it was called a Quonset hut. It was like a long, low hotel room with a hobbity roof. At one end were eight narrow cots. Total had instantly claimed one for himself and Akila. I looked away. Nudge wouldn't need hers now.

We had just barely rolled out of our cots when we heard a bang on the metal door. "Ensign Chad Workman reporting for duty!" someone yelled.

I opened the door. "What," I said coldly.

The young crew-cut guy looked startled. He double-checked the number on our door. "Uh, Ensign Workman reporting for duty. I'm supposed to lead some temporary recruits to mess, kit, and then the BSSTC grounds."

I looked back into the dark hut. "Time for the BS, guys!" I glanced at Ensign Workman. "I think we've got the 'mess' thing under our belts. The BS is gonna be up to you."

Ensign Workman was taken aback. "Um, are you hungry? The mess hall is open."

The rest of the flock staggered toward the door and stood in a ruffled, sleepy group behind me. Brigid and John, with their quaint notion of not sleeping in their clothes, were taking longer to get ready.

"We'll bring you some food, Total," I said as he trotted out the door.

"Yeah. This ain't exactly France," Total muttered, heading off to find a good potty spot. He had loved how many French restaurants allowed dogs.

Ensign Workman stared at him, then looked back at me, chuckling nervously. "And after breakfast, we'll get you set up in some uniforms."

Iggy fingered the khaki cloth of his uniform pants. "This is not a good color for me. I'm really more of a 'winter.'"

Frankly, it wasn't a good color on any of us. And it was downright odd on Fang, who normally wore only dark clothes. I was glad, though, that Nudge wasn't here asking if her uniform came in cute pink camo or had a matching headband.

Ensign Workman gasped audibly when I pulled out a pocketknife and started slashing long slits in the backs of our new shirts.

"You're defacing property of the United States Navy!" he said, shocked.

"Gotta let the wings out, man," said Iggy.

Gazzy took no pity on Ensign Workman and proceeded to snap his wings out, right there. Ten feet of authority-defying feathers and bones, attached to a grinning mutant bird kid.

Ensign Workman turned white, which, as you can imagine, only made his uniform look even worse.

The BS grounds were separated from the rest of the base by a seven-foot chain-link fence. A tall, chisel-faced man stood at the entrance, holding a clipboard and wearing a frown. Ensign Workman silently turned us over to him, then slunk away, no doubt hoping never to see us again. It's weird how many people feel that way about us.

"The classroom is aft of those trees!" the guy barked. "March!"

I know this will surprise you, but we're not good marchers. We're not even good at staying in line. And if you've skimmed any of my previous adventures, you've already figured out how well we respond to orders.

Of any kind.

33

I WAS ALREADY SEETHING as we trooped through the doors into a small, linoleum-tiled classroom. A *classroom.* People trying to stick me in classrooms was becoming as predictable and annoying as people trying to kill me, but with less-fun results.

"I can't believe I'm sitting at a freaking *desk* when my mom is tied up on a submarine somewhere!" I exploded. "This is total crap!"

"Sit down!" snapped our instructor.

With great difficulty, I forced myself to sit on a plastic chair attached to a metal desk. I was calculating how much force I'd need to hurl one of these desks through a window when several other students, male and female, dressed in khaki, looking young and impressionable, filed in silently and immediately took their seats. They tried hard to ignore us, already well on their way to the whole stiff-upper-lip thing, but I felt them sneaking glances.

The man was writing on the whiteboard at the front of the classroom. "LTC Palmer."

He dropped some files on the desk and turned to regard the class with loathing.

Angel raised her hand. "Excuse me. What does LTC stand for?" She blinked innocently. You know and I know that Angel is two parts adorable blond cherub, two parts unholy demon, and two parts of something completely indefinable but even scarier. Most people only see the cute little girl. The lucky ones.

"Loving Tender Care?" Gazzy suggested.

If our instructor had had lasers for eyes (like Flyboys did, for example, or the latest dumb-bots we'd battled, the M-Geeks), he would have sliced Gazzy in half.

"Lieutenant colonel," he sputtered. "You're here to learn how to survive, kid. Why, I don't know. But it's my job to teach you. First lesson: you speak only when spoken to. You got that?"

Okay, I admit it: I giggled. It's just so dang cute when grown-ups get all bossy. Instantly, the lieutenant colonel's eyes were locked on mine. I swallowed my chuckle and looked at my feet. He turned back to Gazzy.

"*You got that?*"

"Uh-huh," said Gazzy.

"You say, 'Yes, sir!' "

"Okay." Gazzy was starting to get bewildered.

"Say it."

"Oh. Okay. Yes, sir." Gazzy looked pleased with himself.

I had a question. "Why does the name Pearl Harbor sound so familiar?"

The lieutenant colonel's eyes narrowed. "Pearl Harbor is the most famous U.S. military base in the world," he said crisply. "It's the only place on U.S. soil that has been attacked in a war, since the Revolutionary War."

None of this was ringing a bell, but you already know I'm totally uneducated.

Gazzy leaned over to whisper, "It was a movie with Ben Affleck."

Ah. Now I remembered.

The lieutenant colonel turned back to the whiteboard. He wrote, The Basics: Personal Defense. Weapons Use. Outdoor Survival. Covert Operations.

Let's cast our minds back, shall we? The flock is, well, somewhat talented in the area of self-defense. Most weapons we were already pretty familiar with—though, granted, I'd probably need some coaching in launching air missiles. Outdoor survival? You mean, what we'd been doing for the past two years? The desert rats, the cactus smoothies, the hobo packs made of whatever we could steal from Dumpsters? I think we're good there. And of course, covert operations. That was going to be fun. I could hardly wait till they saw Fang disappear right before their eyes.

I figured we could knock this course off by about four o'clock this afternoon, if we took a short lunch. Then we could get on an official U.S. Navy vessel and *go spring my mom at long last!*

Then I was going to take Mr. Chu apart, one piece at a time, and feed him to the weirdly enthusiastic seabirds that seemed to hang out here.

34

I LEANED OVER the instructor, looking anxiously at his face. "You okay? Sorry. Didn't mean to slam you against the wall that hard. Nose not broken? Good."

The guy in the white karate gi, his black belt marked with eight level lines, was still trying to catch his breath. He'd already tried jackknifing to his feet, only to slide slowly sideways as his brain realized that his lungs didn't have any oxygen in them.

We stood around waiting, along with the rest of the class, which now stared at us as if we were freaks. Oh, wait—that was because we *are*.

So far in this class, there had been ten minutes of watching the instructor chop, flip, throw, kick, and punch just about everyone in the room. He'd ignored us until I'd stepped right in front of him, ready to take my turn in line.

"You can just watch for now," he'd said briskly.

I shook my head. "Let's get it over with."

So he'd explained what he was going to do and how I should block it or evade it, but I was already thinking about lunch and didn't really pay attention. Then he'd come at me, and I dodged to one side, under his arm, then kicked his knee out from in back, making him sag.

He started to spin, but I gave him a two-handed chop on the shoulder, trying not to break his collarbone, then jumped and did a spinning back kick, right into his chest. That was when he'd smacked up against the wall and slid down like a raindrop.

He looked a little better now, wheezing slightly and sitting up.

"I told ol' Palmer that we had a pretty good handle on this, but I guess he didn't believe me," I said apologetically.

His eyes narrowed as he slowly stood up, a good six inches taller than me, and I'm five-eight. He probably outweighed me by about a hundred and forty pounds. "That was a fluke," he said. "I was going easy on you because you're a kid. But if you want a fight, I can fight."

I guess this gets filed in the bulging folder of Max's Nongirliness, but my heart gave a little jump. I'd been worried about getting soft, losing my razor-sharp survival instincts. And what do you know, this nice navy guy was volunteering to help me brush up on them.

"Yeah?" I said, trying not to look too excited. Behind me, I heard Fang snort, saw Gazzy and Iggy start to calculate odds and exchange money.

"Don't hurt him too bad, Max," said Angel, smothering a grin as fury crossed the instructor's face. He rolled his shoulders, walked about ten paces away, and cracked his knuckles. The other students looked nervous and backed away from us, edging toward the door.

He stared at me with cold, cut-me-no-slack determination, then got into a fighting stance, holding one hand out, beckoning me.

"I saw that movie too!" I said. "It was like the coolest movie of all—"

He launched himself at me.

That was when his day really went downhill.

It didn't last that long—maybe four minutes. Which can feel like a long time when someone's whaling on you. Not to malign the U.S. Navy or anything, but he didn't land a single blow. Maybe he was having an off day. Finally, we resumed our earlier position: me leaning over him as he gasped on the floor.

"It's not your fault," I said, not even breathing hard. "I'm genetically enhanced. And, you know, ruthless. Plus, of course, meaner than a rabid wolverine. Are you okay?"

After a long pause, he nodded silently.

I jerked a thumb at the rest of the flock. "Do you want to try it against any of them?"

Everyone except Fang failed at not looking hopeful. The guy shook his head no.

"Good choice. Then how about you give us a checkmark saying we passed the self-defense part of the BS? Okay?"

He nodded again.

I looked at the others. "Is it lunchtime yet? I'm starving."

Iggy felt his watch. "It's a little past nine. In the morning," he clarified.

I groaned. "Okay, let's find some vending machines. I need, like, about a million Twinkies."

It looked like we might be finished by four, after all.

35

Q: You're presented with a smooth-faced, eight-foot-high wooden wall. Your objective? Get over it. To, like, save comrades or something. How to accomplish this?

A: Take a running start, brace one foot against the wall, throw one hand to the top, try to hang on long enough for a comrade to either grab your hand at the top or for another comrade to push your butt over from below. It takes teamwork!

BKA (bird-kid answer): Or, you could just, like, *fly* over it.

Q: Twenty yards of dirt to crawl across on your belly. The catch? Rows and rows of barbed wire, strung eighteen inches off the ground. How do you get across without being snagged?

A: Do the "sniper" crawl. Be sure not to raise your butt or shoulders or head too high. Ouch.

BKA: What can I say? We've been crawling like rats and slithering like snakes for years. How else to sneak up on each other, hiding beneath the bed frame to grab Iggy's ankle when he gets up for a drink of water? Plus, we're really thin. If we keep our wings tucked in tight, no worries.

Q: Is there anything a bird kid can't do?

A: No. Apparently not.

BKA: Well, we still totally fall down in the table-manners department. I'm just saying.

Rope swings over quicksand, wading through rivers while holding weapons above our heads, balancing on spinning logs, climbing ropes, running fast, crawling through tunnels—we were starting to seriously depress our fellow naval classmates, all of whom were older than us and had already been in training for a while.

Explaining that we'd been designed to be strong, fast, and light didn't really cheer them up. They just saw us kids beating the socks off them. We were barely panting when our classmates were bent over at the knees, throwing up from exertion. Heights don't bother us. (Duh.) We've already been in awful, to-the-death fights. We've already been chained in dungeons. Locked in dog crates and experimented on. We've crawled through miles of air-conditioning ducts. Been pushed to our extreme limits physically, psychologically, emotionally. All of this BS training was just kind of a picnic after that.

Is that what Jeb had meant when he said everything that we've gone through was just a way to train me for the future? I would *so* hate for him to be right.

"This is fun!" Gazzy exclaimed, shoveling down the food at lunchtime. "That obstacle course reminded me of that time when we were jacking the car from the chop shop, remember? And we had to climb through all those piles of car parts without making a sound? Pass the ketchup."

I pushed the ketchup his way.

"I gotta hand it to the navy," said Iggy. "They know how to keep the chow coming." He got up to get fourths, easily threading his way through the tables and the crowd, picking up a fresh tray and starting again at the beginning of the line.

"Okay, are we done yet?" I asked Fang. "It's almost one o'clock. My mom has been tied up on a sub for almost two days! Every minute counts here!"

"We've gotten through self-defense, the obstacle course, and outdoor survival," said Fang. "We've still got weapons use. We'll probably be done by five or so."

"What's next?" Angel asked, starting on her third hamburger.

Fang checked our list. "Covert ops."

Angel smiled.

36

“TAG! YOU’RE IT!” Gazzy tapped the navy guy on the shoulder, causing him to jump about a foot in the air and stifle a shriek.

I have to admit, it was almost fun being set loose in a patch of heavily palm-treed terrain and then having to get past guards to get to “home base.”

Fang pretty much just walked past the camouflaged guards, taking slow, quiet steps, pacing his breathing, and simply blending in with the trees.

Iggy and I had been forced into more stealthiness, actually ducking behind trees and the occasional huge volcanic boulder. All the same, despite the wide-eyed alertness of the sailors on guard, it really wasn’t too hard to slither past them in a big circle.

Gazzy had relied on the element of surprise, as he often does. First, he'd perfectly mimicked a bird call, making a guard look up. Gazzy had tagged that guard. Then, when the guards were in pursuit, he'd utilized his other—well, I refuse to call it a skill. In fact, I think of it as a huge design flaw. Despite how hilarious the guys think it is, Nudge and Angel and I are simply more evolved than that. We try not to encourage demonstrations of his mastery of the gaseous arts.

Suffice it to say that Gazzy incapacitated the guards, leaving them coughing and gagging, gasping on the ground, their eyes watering. Then he raced through the trees, cackling in triumph, and burst out into the clear meadow where the lieutenant colonel was waiting with a clipboard and a stopwatch.

Iggy and Fang gave Gazzy high fives just as Lieutenant Colonel Palmer's nose turned up, and he frowned at the woods.

"It'll dissipate in a couple minutes," I said, flopping down on the grass. "It always does."

Palmer turned a ferocious glare on Gazzy. "You were forbidden to bring or to use antipersonnel weapons!"

"That's the sad thing," I said, just as Angel trotted out of the woods. "He didn't. I mean, his *name* is the *Gasman*. We're not just whistling Dixie, there."

"Am I the last one?" Angel asked as she got near. "Sorry. Got sidetracked by some wild orchids." She handed me a small bouquet of creamy flowers.

"Ooh, thanks, sweetie," I said, inhaling their delicate scent. "So. Time for weapons class?"

The lieutenant colonel glared first at me, then at Angel. The two guards staggered out of the woods, still holding their rifles, but with their helmets askew and their camo gear trailing behind them.

"Ensigns Baker and Kipowski!" Palmer barked. "All five of these recruits exited the woods within four minutes! Did you see them?"

Looking dazed, the ensigns tried to straighten up. One of them cleared his throat. "We didn't see the tall dark one, sir, or the tall blond one, or the oldest girl. We saw the younger boy, but he... incapacitated us."

Palmer just stared at them.

Gazzy stifled a snicker. "Burritos for lunch," he whispered, and Iggy and Fang tried to hold in their laughter.

"What about this one?" Palmer pointed his pen at Angel, who gave him a sunny smile.

The guards looked at her, and confusion crossed their faces.

I tried not to groan.

"I think I saw her," one said slowly. "I don't remember."

"You don't—" Palmer seemed speechless. I knew it couldn't last.

"I might have seen her," said the other guard, his eyes on the ground. "I just—it's all—I don't know."

I stood up and brushed off my khaki butt. "I guess it's time for weapons class," I said pointedly.

Palmer was still staring at the two guards. I went over to him.

"Lieutenant Colonel," I said. "Can I call you L? No? Well, look, it's not their fault. They probably would have caught anyone else. But we're good at this stuff. As I keep telling you."

"She's a child!" Palmer burst out, gesturing at Angel.

"She's a sneaky and devious child," I explained. "Plus, you know, I think she zapped the guards. With her mind. She can hear people's thoughts and sometimes control them. It's weird, it's scary, but there you go. Your guys never had a chance."

The lieutenant colonel seemed less comforted by my explanation than you might think. Finally, he let his clipboard dangle at his side. "Weapons class," he said. But you could tell his heart wasn't really in it anymore.

37

LIEUTENANT COLONEL PALMER, still looking tense from the demoralizing covert ops training, stood at the front of the classroom. He opened a case on the desk and took out a James Bond–like handgun.

"This is the Beretta M9, a semiautomatic pistol," he said, being careful not to point it at anyone. "It's one of the safest and best-designed handguns in the world and is standard issue for several branches of the U.S. military."

Gazzy raised his hand.

The lieutenant colonel seemed to go a little pale but ignored him. "Capable of handling fifteen-round magazines, this weapon has proved to be one of the most reliable and accurate—"

Gazzy waved his hand back and forth. Impossible to ignore.

Palmer tried looking stern. “This better be good, son,” he said, gritting his teeth.

“The Beretta is great and all,” said Gazzy earnestly, “but I’ve heard the military-issued model tends to jam something awful. People think it’s the weird finish on the barrels. Plus, it’s supposedly really heavy, bowling ball heavy. Kind of like the all-steel M1911 model. And then the trigger’s too far away for most people, even if they have big hands...”

Lieutenant Colonel Palmer was nonplussed. Again.

Gazzy looked at him, concerned. “Um, it’s still a really neat gun, though,” he said. “And did you know—if you stick the spring from a clothespin right under the safety when it’s in the left-hand mode, then pull the trigger, it’ll explode about two-point-nine seconds later? I mean, *throw* it first.”

“Sometimes two-point-seven seconds,” Iggy added. “Don’t dawdle. And man—try doing that with the barrel full of Spam sometime!” He and Gazzy chortled and slapped high fives.

About a minute later, the lieutenant colonel rubbed his eyes. “Class dismissed.”

38

LIEUTENANT KHAKI, whose name was actually Lieutenant Morgan, sat at her desk, reading Lieutenant Colonel Palmer's report. Every once in a while she looked up at us sharply, as if she were having trouble believing it. Finally she put it down and laced her fingers together.

"So you're saying these children can easily run four miles carrying heavy packs?"

"Yes, ma'am," said the lieutenant colonel, looking straight ahead. The flock and I were lined up against one wall.

"They outperformed the rest of the cadets in every way?"

"Yes, ma'am."

"The eight-year-old beat your best cadet in hand-to-hand combat?"

"So did the six-year-old girl, ma'am. Actually, she beat the instructor also."

I tried not to grin. The self-defense instructor had given all of us a pass, but the hand-to-hand combat instructor had been more stubborn. For a while.

"So, like, we want to thank you for this great experience..." I began, shifting from foot to foot. "But now that we've gone through all your BS, can we go rescue my mom?"

The lieutenant looked at me. "Yes," she said finally, and my heart leaped. "Tomorrow."

"What?!"

"We're putting you on the USS *Minnesota,*" she went on smoothly. "Which is a state-of-the-art, Virginia-class nuclear submarine with many enhanced offensive and defensive capabilities. It's on its way here now from San Diego. It will arrive here at oh-three-hundred hours tomorrow, will refuel, and be ready to deploy at oh-six-hundred hours. You will be waiting on the dock at that time. If you are two minutes late, it will leave without you. In addition, while on board the USS *Minnesota,* you will obey every senior officer without question, you will comport yourself with decorum and maturity, and you will do nothing to endanger the ship, its cargo, or its personnel."

I opened my mouth to say something, but the lieutenant plowed on. "Failure to follow these rules to the letter will result in your being disembarked at the closest possible location, and the mission will be scrubbed. Do I make myself perfectly clear?"

Her icy blue eyes raked each of us one by one. I prayed that the others would stifle their trademark lack of respect and intolerance for bull and, for once, keep their mouths shut. My mom's life was riding on this.

Then, a miracle happened. No one said a word. I heard cautious, even breathing as each of us bit our lips and struggled mightily against our true natures.

Don't wait too long, I begged the lieutenant silently. *Please dismiss us before we blurt out something bad, against our will.*

"Oh-six-hundred hours then," she said curtly. "Dismissed."

39

SO WHAT DO YOU DO if you have thirteen hours to kill before you rescue your mom? Well, if you're wacky, devil-may-care bird kids, you go swimming!

Pearl Harbor was in a bay off the coast of Oahu, *this close* to Honolulu. In fact, *Honolulu* means "sheltered bay," according to a little sign by the mess hall. (See? Who says you never learn nothin', hanging out with us?)

Some of the shoreline near the base was off-limits, but there was a public part too. Despite it being early evening, the weather was perfect and balmy, and the water was blissfully warm. The beach wasn't crowded, but there were people swimming and collecting shells. I was starting to see Fang's point about just finding a tropical isle and letting the rest of the world go crazy without us.

"Keep your Windbreaker on," I told Angel, who was shimmying out of her tiny uniform. "Bird kids weren't exactly designed for bathing suits."

She made a face but nodded. "I think there's like dolphins or something out there. I can hear things thinking, but they're not human."

Concern shot through me. "Not human? Do they feel evil? They're not, like, Erasers with fins or something, right?"

Angel giggled. "No. They're not Erasers. And they feel totally not evil. Okay, bye!" She ran across the sand and threw herself into the water. I watched as her golden curls submerged and disappeared. I sighed and sank down on the sand next to Akila and Total.

Fang sat next to me, still looking out of character in nonblack clothes.

"Whoa. Khaki much?" I couldn't resist saying.

He looked at me. "Uh-huh. And I dig your military hair."

"Touché." Self-consciously, I touched the tight French braid I was required to wear here at the navy fun house.

Gazzy and Iggy were already in swimming trunks, racing toward the ocean. They yelled when they hit the waves, plunging in far enough to bodysurf.

Fang's dark eyes scanned the water. He was counting heads, the way I was. I hadn't gotten over the feeling that something was wrong because Nudge wasn't here.

"How long's she been under?" Fang asked.

"About five minutes. She said there were dolphins. Or something."

We sat together silently for a while. Gazzy and Iggy were shouting and splashing in the water. Angel still hadn't come up for air, and I tried to let go of the normal expectation that she needed to. After all, what are a few gills among friends?

Suddenly Angel did pop up, smiling and waving, heading toward us. "It's totally awesome, clear and blue," she announced, shaking off water.

"Were there dolphins?" I asked.

She nodded. "Yeah. They're really mad. Hey, Total. Come out with me. Practice breathing under water."

Total wrinkled his nose. "No gills," he said. "And I'm still getting used to the wings."

I was stuck on the angry dolphins, but Angel frowned at Total, then at me and Fang. "You guys all really need to practice breathing under water," she said urgently. "It's really important. I want you to practice right now."

"Sweetie, I don't think any of us can breathe under water except you," I said. "Remember when Gazzy tried? He barfed up half the ocean. And what do you mean, the dolphins are mad?"

"I really think you guys should try," Angel said, wearing her familiar and dreaded "I'm not gonna let this go" expression. "You might have developed gills by now."

"Don't think so," I said. "Now, back to the angry dolphins—"

A piercing scream stopped me, and Fang and I leaped to our feet.

A woman was standing at the edge of the ocean, pointing frantically at a small boy being swept out to sea. "A riptide got him!" the woman screamed. "Someone help him! Call nine-one-one!" She plunged into the water but stopped when it reached her waist.

Gazzy and Iggy had set off after the kid, but the tide had pulled him amazingly far out in just a few moments. Fang and I looked at each other, then whipped off our jackets at the same time. Ignoring all the bystanders, we sped across the sand. Right as we reached the small cresting waves of the ocean, we snapped out our wings and jumped up into the air.

Working powerfully, we raced low over the water. The spray misted my face, the wind whipped through my hair, and I could smell the salt air. We were flying again. It felt like we hardly ever got a chance to anymore.

We were incredibly fast, but not fast enough. When we were almost there, the boy sank beneath the waves, his small arms still reaching up. In an instant, we angled down sharply, folding back our wings, and hit the water.

It was so clear that we immediately saw the kid's bright red rash-guard shirt. His eyes were closed, his face still and pale in the aqua light. We each grabbed an arm, then shot up toward the surface with as much force as we could, popping out of the water like corks, hoping we could get airborne.

It worked. Our wings brushed against each other, but we managed to get aloft and streaked back to land. Sadly, our landing was less than graceful because of our shared cargo, but we thunked to a stop in the sand without falling and put the boy down.

"I know CPR!" a man shouted, already kneeling. Within less than a minute, the little boy was gagging and retching, then gasping for air. "Mom?" he choked out, and then the woman hauled him into her arms. They were both crying, holding each other tight.

Fang and I faded back to where the flock was waiting with Total and Akila.

Angel looked at us accusingly. "You didn't even practice breathing under water just now, did you?"

40

WHAT THE HECK—everyone had already seen the wings, so there was no point waiting for the tram to take us back to Navy Central. Instead, the six of us hit the skies, the warm breeze sticking our sodden clothes to our bodies. Total flew alongside me, still awkward with the whole flapping thing. He was getting better, though. Iggy and Fang took turns carrying Akila, who was eighty pounds of hot fur. Total talked to her reassuringly, but she was not thrilled to be this high up.

It took about two minutes to get back to the base, and we came down on the training field, landing smoothly and lightly in front of about a hundred stunned ensigns. The next thing we knew, John Abate, Brigid

Dwyer, and Lieutenant Colonel Palmer were hurrying toward us.

"You're heroes!" John said, waving. "We just heard about your daring sea rescue."

I stared. "How did you hear so quickly?"

"We have you under surveillance. For safety reasons," said the lieutenant colonel stiffly. Actually, he seemed incapable of speaking in any other way, so from now on, if he talks, assume it's "stiffly" and I'll quit putting that in, okay?

"Oh, for Pete's sake," I muttered, heading off to our hut to change.

"Fang!" said Brigid, pushing past me. "I can't believe you risked your life for that little boy! You're wonderful!"

I gazed openmouthed as Brigid gave Fang a big bear hug, wrapping her arms around him. I was about to say, "I risked *my* life too," but then realized I didn't want her to hug me. And I didn't want to look petty. And the truth was, the rescue had been a snap, compared to other situations, like when Angel and the dogs had been trapped in an ice crevasse in Antarctica. Or when we'd all been in a huge cage, and my half brother, Ari, had literally chewed his way through its metal bars to set us free. For example.

Today we hadn't risked anything except the possibility of our new jeans shrinking up on us. My jaw set in disgust as I stalked past them, my stomach clenching at the sight of Brigid pressed against Fang like ugly on an ape.

"You must come have dinner with us at the Officer's Mess," Brigid gushed.

"Uh, I'm busy," Fang muttered.

My eyes widened, but I kept walking and refused to turn around. That's me: suave Max.

"Hey," Fang said, falling into step with me. I looked at him. "We have to eat. Let's you and me go into town. I'll treat you to the best artery-clogging Hawaiian food we can find."

My heart began thudding painfully inside my chest. I wondered if Fang could hear it. "You mean the whole flock?" I asked casually, trying not to shriek with tension.

"Nah. They can eat at the Officer's Mess with Brigid and John," he said.

I stopped and looked into his eyes, seeing nothing but my own reflection, as usual. "Just you and me?" I repeated, barely hanging on to my suavity by my fingernails.

His eyes were unreadable. "Yeah."

"Hawaiian food?"

"Yeah."

I was still grossed out by the Brigid display and wanted to coolly brush past him with a mild, "I'll think about it." But the combination of having Fang all to myself, plus fun food, was rapidly pummeling my self-respect into the dust. Then I remembered something.

"The last time we . . . left the flock, all heck broke loose," I reminded him.

He grinned, one of those rare Fang grins that lights up his face and makes the sun stop in its tracks.

"This time they're protected by the U.S. Navy," he pointed out.

I laughed, relief flooding through me. "Well, okay. You got me there." Oh, boy, did he have me.

41

WAS THIS A DATE? Those four words kept swirling through my mind, over and over, and it was getting to the point where I wanted the old Voice back, just for a change of pace, to hear someone who at least pretended to be rational.

Which I so wasn't. The whole thing was like a dream. All I knew was that we were in Honolulu. There were festive streetlights and store windows everywhere, crowds of people walking past, many sailors in uniform, an ocean, kind of all around us, and...

Me and Fang. Holding hands and eating ice cream.

And the flock was safe on a giant naval base where you couldn't even spit without hitting an antiaircraft missile.

If life got better than this, I didn't think I could take it.

I wanted time to stand still, and not in the creepy,

someone-injected-drugs-into-my-brain-so-time-has-become-meaningless kind of way but just...every second had weight. My skin was tingling, my brain was racing, and everything seemed extra whatever it was. Extrafun. Extrabeautiful. Extrayummy.

The hand holding Fang's seemed to have three times as many sense receptors, and I hoped it wasn't some new ability showing up. I was still worried about gills appearing.

This totally felt like a date.

And the beautiful part? He'd turned down Dr. Stupendous to be with *moi*. He'd dissed her and dismissed her, so he could eat kimchi and ice cream with yours featherly.

"Max?"

I suddenly became aware that Fang had said my name like three times. Now he stopped and looked at me. "Are you okay? Is the Voice back, giving you instructions?"

"Uh-huh. It's in the middle of the crossword of the day."

He smiled, and we kept walking.

"No, I was just spacing out," I said, licking my ice cream. I had gotten a double scoop of mint chocolate chip and orange sherbet, two great tastes that tasted great together.

"Well, tomorrow we leap into action," he said. "So, last chance to space out for a while."

"Yeah. I just hope—"

"I know. I'm sure she's okay. We'll get there in time. And I promise to let you take her kidnappers apart all by yourself."

He knew me so well. "Thanks. It's just—it's bad enough to worry about the flock. Is Nudge okay, is everyone here, are we together, are we safe? I can't stand the circle getting bigger. I can only worry about so much before my head explodes, you know?"

He nodded. "You know I got your back. You're not alone."

I couldn't speak for a moment, so I swallowed hard and cleaned up a drip making its way down my sugar cone. "Thanks," I said finally. "I know." Suddenly we were at a metal railing, looking out at water. "Oh! Is this the ocean?"

"It keeps cropping up. What with the islandness and all."

Fang dropped my hand to put his arm around my shoulders, his warmth searing my skin through my jacket. I really, really hoped that I hadn't suddenly sprouted a catrillion new nerve endings. Yes, it would make moments like this better, but the downside? Pain and torture would be a million times worse. Guess which one I was more likely to come up against?

I finished my cone, sucking the ice cream out of the hole in the bottom before I realized how tacky and ungirl-like that was. Oops. I wiped my hands on my jeans and looked out at the deep blue water, glistening with moonlight, knowing that somewhere my mom was being held captive beneath it.

Then I realized that despite everything, I felt... happy?

Safe? Complete? I didn't know what to call it. It wasn't something that I was on familiar terms with. I just knew I didn't want this night to end.

I mean, I *did*, of course—because when the night ended, we would finally, finally, *finally* go save my mom.

But besides that, I didn't want this night to end.

"Max." Fang put two fingers under my chin—I hoped it wasn't sticky but wasn't sure—and gently turned me to face him. "You're a million miles away again."

"Sorry." Once more I cursed Jeb for not grafting the gift of gab into my DNA. Jerk.

"Are you too worried about your mom? Do you want to head back?"

"No," I said, meeting his gaze. "No. I'm okay. Just—kind of overwhelmed." I gave a little cough. "I don't want to go back. I want to be here with you."

Something lit in his black eyes. "Yeah?"

I nodded.

"So... you're choosing me?"

Okay, if this is what falling in love feels like, someone please kill me now. (Not literally, overzealous readers.) But it was all too much—too much emotion, too much happiness, too much longing, perhaps too much ice cream...

I had to grip the metal railing hard with both hands so I wouldn't throw myself over it, to streak away into the night, into darkness and safety. *Tough it out, Max,* I told myself—or maybe it was the Voice.

But it didn't matter, because then Fang leaned down

and kissed me, and I put my arms around him, right there in front of everyone, and kissed him back with everything I had.

And then, all heck broke loose.

Of course.

Because this is *my* life, right?

42

"I MISS HER, but...it's kind of *nice* not having Nudge around being all goody-goody," Gazzy whispered as they quietly shut the Quonset hut door behind them.

"How can you say that? I totally miss her." Angel breathed. "Oh—guards ahead at two o'clock. Let's detour."

Iggy, Gazzy, and Angel pressed themselves into the shadows as MPs carrying rifles marched by on their rounds. When the MPs were out of earshot, the three bird kids hustled across the training field to the high fence, then nimbly flew over it and headed to the beach, well below any radar.

When they'd landed on the sand, Gazzy continued. "I miss Nudge too—a lot. But you know she was always the one who'd be like, 'We better ask Max. Maybe we shouldn't do this. Are you sure that's okay?' and stuff." Gazzy had mimicked Nudge's voice so perfectly that the other two, for a split second, expected to see her standing right there next to them.

"Well, Nudge isn't here," said Iggy, kicking off his shoes. "I wish she was, annoying caution and all. But since she isn't"—he turned and grinned—"we can try the super-duper-oxygen-scoopers!" He held up a couple of contraptions that consisted of pilfered scuba masks, a vacuum cleaner hose, the motor from a blender, and some charcoal briquettes.

Gazzy held out his hand. "Super-duper-oxygen-scooper, please," he said solemnly. He and Iggy each donned a contraption.

"You guys should really just try breathing under water," Angel said, her hands on her hips. "It's really important! Just try!"

"The last time I tried, I hurled for half an hour," Gazzy said, his voice muffled by the tube in his mouth. "Max still won't swim in that stretch of ocean off the East Coast. Nope, for me, it's the latest handy-dandy *inventionuoso* by that brilliant duo of mutant scientists: Iggy and the Gasman! Who have genius programmed right in!"

Angel rolled her eyes behind her goggles, which Gazzy could easily see in the bright moonlight. Then she jumped upward, spread her pure-white wings, and flew out over the water. Gazzy and Iggy followed her.

When they were about a quarter mile from shore, they all folded back their wings, and dove in.

Even at night, with their raptor eyesight, they could see a whole different world under water, and set off to explore.

The super-duper-oxygen-scoopers worked as planned, siphoning ocean water through some filters, separating the air out, and shunting it into the boys' mouths. Gazzy took Iggy's hand and touched it to his own, which was making a triumphant thumbs-up. Iggy nodded enthusiastically.

Look! Sharks!

Angel's thought floated into Gazzy's brain, and for a second he was jealous that his own flesh-and-blood-and-feather sister could do that and he couldn't. But his head swiveled until he saw Iggy pointing to the left. His heart quickened as he saw the enormous hammerhead shark seeming to glide lazily through the water.

Iggy took the rebreather out of his mouth. "I can sort of see down here!" His words were bubbly and indistinct, but Gazzy and Angel could make them out. "It's like my echolocation works superwell!" He grinned hugely, then put his rebreather back in. "Oh. Big sharks."

Again Gazzy turned to see several more hammerheads slowly undulating through the water. He was close enough to see their weirdly dead-looking eyes, and he shivered. Meeting Angel's glance, he signaled to her: *make them go away.* She nodded, looking disappointed, then fastened her gaze on the huge fish.

It took several moments, and Gazzy had no idea what she told them, but the sharks gradually drifted away. Breathing a bubbly sigh of relief, Gazzy swam toward the large coral reef. He almost wished he could live under water all the time. It was so peaceful. There were so many amazing things to see—starfish clinging to the reef, a million different kinds of fish, some of them tiny and brilliantly colored, and some of them—

"Waugh!" Gazzy shouted into his rebreather. Right next to him, about three times as big as he is, was an enormous silver fish, its body shaped like a gigantic silver dollar rimmed with bright orange red fins.

The fish looked at him. Gazzy, frozen, looked back. The fish seemed to tilt its head to one side, puzzling over Gazzy, who could hardly breathe.

Angel swam up, smiling. She reached out her hand and stroked the shiny silver side. The fish seemed to enjoy it and turned to her. Angel tickled under its chin. Gazzy could swear that it grinned. Slowly he stretched out his own hand and patted the fish's side. It was smooth and cool, with tiny ruffled scales. It was like a big fish-dog, practically wagging its tail fin with delight.

Then two things happened: First, several sudden, searing strings brushed against Gazzy's face and arms, causing him to shriek and almost lose the rebreather. And then Iggy shouted: "Sharks! Sharks! And they're bloody!"

The pain on his face and arms was so intense, Gazzy felt like he might pass out. But through the bloody water, he could blearily see the hammerheads thrashing, eating something big and white.

At that moment several of the enormous predators turned and spotted Iggy, Angel, and Gazzy. They no longer looked calm and placid. They looked sharp, powerful, fast, and hungry. With jaws agape to reveal rows of razor-sharp teeth, they whipped their long tails back and forth, speeding toward the three bird kids.

43

OKAY, I CONFESS: When I heard the deep, rumbling noises and picked up on the bright flashes, even through my closed eyelids, all I thought was, *Oh, my God. Fang is rocking my world!* Just like those teen magazines say: "Does he put stars in your eyes? Does your heart skip a beat? Does the earth move whenever he's around?"

I was thinking, *Yes, yes, yes! All of those things*!

Then I realized it was partly Fang and partly a bunch of M-Geeks with automatic weapons. The area around me was being strafed with *bullets*. Because this is *me* we're talking about, not some cute teenager with shiny hair, a perfect smile, and *no wings*.

"Duck!" Fang yelled, pushing me to the ground and rolling with me under a cement bench. All around us, bullets sent chips of concrete ricocheting through the air. One shard hit my cheek, and I winced at the sting.

"I knew this was too good to be true," I muttered, and Fang squeezed my side. "You think they know we're here to rescue my mom? Are we getting too close?" Peering out from under our bench, we saw that there weren't that many of the dumb-bots—maybe about twenty. They gave new meaning to the phrase "heavily armed."

As the gang of M-Geeks slowly moved in, closing in a semicircle, all around us people were screaming and running away. Soon we would be surrounded, with just a shot-up bench between us and a bunch of trigger-happy robots grafted with Uzis.

Max the Leader stepped up. "Okay, behind us there's a metal railing, then the cliff, and the ocean," I said to Fang quickly. "Ease backward, beneath the railing, then drop down the cliff face. Wings out, we zoom up, and circle around in back of them."

"Excellent plan," Fang whispered. "Then what?"

"No idea. Start backing."

Fang shot out from beneath the bench, scurrying over the cliff in less than a second. I was right behind him. I felt myself push off from the edge and snapped out my wings, then I was free-falling, praying I wouldn't hit the sharp rocks below before I got some altitude.

The tip of my sneaker brushed one jagged boulder, and then my wings carried me upward, fast and hard. We swooped out low over the ocean, then circled back around the tip of the jetty. I was thinking as fast and hard as I was flying.

"We've got to get them over that cliff," Fang said as we began to come up behind them. They were still closing in on the bench, shooting round after round. The nearby trash can had been peppered with bullets, a sign hung down broken, and the cement bench looked like Swiss cheese. Most important, the metal railing had been shot to pieces and would easily give way.

"Yeah." I frowned. "Aren't they using heat sensors? They don't know we're not there!"

"Maybe they're just programmed to go forward and shoot," Fang said. "Or maybe someone's controlling them remotely, and they can't tell their target is gone."

It was weird. Something felt off. There was a missing piece to this puzzle, and I couldn't figure out what it was. But in the meantime, those 'bots were going overboard.

We came up from behind them, starting way high and then dive-bombing at more than two hundred miles an hour. I loved doing this—it's like being in a video game where you have to recalculate your trajectory ten times a second so you don't hit a building.

A few seconds before we hit them, we swung down in big arcs, our feet out in front of us.

Wham! I slammed into one so hard my teeth rattled. The impact lifted the 'bot almost two feet off the ground, sending it headfirst into the 'bot in front of it. Then it was just a matter of the domino effect.

We backed up as fast as we could and did it again. Before they could focus on us, the first line had already toppled through the shredded railing and dropped thirty feet down onto enormous, sharp-edged rocks. *Ka-boom!*

Only one of them managed to swivel in time to aim at us, but I went in low and kicked out its ankles, sliding on the asphalt and ripping huge holes in my best jeans. It tipped backward and then went over, still spewing bullets.

Cautiously, Fang and I peeked over the edge. Things were still sparking, there were a few lights still on, but there was no way for a heavy machine to survive that fall. With the bazillion dollars it must have cost to develop that technology, you would think that they would make them a little more impact tolerant.

We knew better than to hang around. Already, police cars and fire trucks were screeching to a halt, sirens blaring, lights going berserk. Fang and I raced silently along the edge of the boardwalk, then jumped over the edge, around the corner from where the 'bots had smashed.

Once again we whipped out our wings and soared out to sea, flying low and fast over the water. The balmy night air felt amazing on my face and in my hair.

So let's take stock of the evening, shall we?

Pros: Excellent Hawaiian food, ice cream, making out with Fang (aiieee!!!), and victory against murderous, bird-kid-hating, killing machines.

Cons: Well, the murderous, bird-kid-hating, killing

machines, for one. For another, I looked down and realized that not only had I destroyed my best pair of jeans, but, in fact, they didn't even go with my shirt in the first place. Typical.

Third, there was something dark speeding right toward us. Going as fast as we were. A missile? A rocket? Our night wasn't over yet.

44

THE GASMAN SPIT OUT his regulator and screamed, "Angel!" His face and arms were on fire, and he felt like he was going to barf. Under water. How would that even work?

Suddenly, the sharks were right there, mouths wide open, full of blood and chunks of something, and stretching, reaching, snapping at—

Just water, because Angel was holding up her hand in the universal "Stop shark attack" gesture. She was frowning sternly at the sharks, one hand on her hip.

"Oh no you don't!" she gurgled loudly, right at the three huge man-eaters.

They stopped, and if they'd been on dry land, they would have skidded. As it was, they came to an abrupt, surprised stop, inches away from the three bird kids. Angel shook her finger at them, in the universal gesture for "Bad! Bad shark!"

Gaz, Ig—you guys back away really slowly.

Gazzy *did* hear that part of Angel's message, so he touched Iggy's hand and, gently, they let themselves drift backward. Gazzy put the regulator back in his mouth, feeling like his lungs were about to burst from lack of air.

Looking sheepish, the hammerheads slowly turned and glided back to their group. Once there, they joined in the feeding frenzy again.

Gosh, they were big, Angel thought to Gazzy and Iggy.

Gazzy nodded, trying not to cry from the pain in his face and arms.

We need to get you out of here, Angel went on sympathetically. *You got stung by something. Can you do a burst out of the water to get airborne?*

Gazzy had felt a lot of pain in his life, but this was different—a horrible, searing sensation, as if someone were holding a lit match to his face and arms. Under water. He nodded bravely to Angel, hoping he wouldn't shriek when the warm air made the burning feel worse.

Okay, then, Angel commanded Gazzy and Iggy. *Hunch down, gather your strength, then burst up through the water as hard as you can. As soon as you're in the air, snap your wings out. Okay?*

On any other day, Gazzy would have said, "Who died and made you Max?" But, all things considered, he could barely think straight. He was thankful that Angel was taking charge. He managed to nod again, then concentrated on balling up his muscles.

One! Two! Three!

Gazzy's face mask was filling with tears, but he hunched down and surged toward the surface. When he broke through the water, he stretched out his wings, pushing down and pulling up as hard as he could.

He rose in the air slowly at first, then powerfully and fast, relief beginning to wash over him.

Only to collide hard with something huge, right above him.

Oof! Gazzy let out a strangled cry—it felt like his face and arms were splitting open—then he felt himself falling.

And this time, he didn't think he'd manage to save himself.

45

RAPTOR VISION ALLOWS US to see tiny things from great heights and to see incredibly well in the dark and in much more detail than regular people. But, for the life of me, I couldn't tell what that thing was, shooting toward us.

"If it's heat-seeking, we should go under water," Fang said tensely. "It'll still get us, but maybe some poor whale or dolphin will confuse it."

Great. A lovely choice. I squinted, wishing the rolling bank of thick gray clouds hadn't totally covered the moon. But—wait...

"Fang—that thing has wings. Is it like an albatross? What's the biggest seabird there is?"

Fang frowned and tilted his head. "Uh—what kind of seabird wears preppy Top-Siders?"

My eyes went wide as I stared first at Fang, then at the dark thing. "Oh, my God! It *is* wearing Top-Siders! It's *Nudge!*" 'Cause, I mean, how many preppy mutant bird kids are there? Not a lot.

Fang and I poured on the speed, scanning the whole sky as we streaked toward Nudge, my *Nudge!* Nothing seemed to be pursuing her; she was flying fast but not panicky. Now we were close enough to see her long ringlets streaming out in back of her, her bright white smile shining in the deep night sky.

My heart swelled, and I admitted to myself just how much I'd missed her, how worried I'd been, how hurt I'd felt that she'd chosen safety, calm, and education over *us*.

"Nudge!" I shrieked, and she beamed and waved.

Just then, something huge shot out of the water and slammed into her. It shoved her off balance, knocking the wind out of her. Fang and I surged forward, going into battle mode, and then *two more things* shot out of the water as if launched from a huge slingshot.

Two large, wet, familiar things.

"Max!"

"Angel?!"

"Get Gazzy! He's hurt! Oh—Nudge?!"

"Angel—hi!"

Fang swooped down and scooped up Gazzy, who had some weird contraption hanging off his head. His eyes were closed, and his face looked like a bulldozer had run over it.

"He's hurt!" Angel said again. "Nudge! I can't believe you're back!"

Here's what I was feeling: elation about seeing Nudge again, alive and unhurt; worry over Gazzy, who was now unconscious as we raced back to the naval base; a guilty thrill over what was happening between me and Fang (*when will it happen again?*); lingering anxiety about my mom; and a deep, abiding contentment that we were all together again, the six of us, my flock, my family.

Not bad, for someone who *hates emotions*.

46

IT TURNED OUT that Gazzy had been stung by a Portuguese man-of-war, an incredibly dangerous and even deadly jellyfish.

"Actually, it's not a real jellyfish," the navy doctor explained. "So its toxins are different, and we treat it differently."

"I offered to pee on him, but they said no," Iggy said, sounding disappointed.

The navy doctor smiled. "That was once thought to be acceptable treatment. Vinegar too. But actually, it's most important to remove any tentacles to prevent further discharge of venom. Rinsing the sting thoroughly with salt water can help."

All of us bird kids have had days when we looked like

we'd been put in a blender set to "whip." As many fights as we've been in, as many hard places we've been—odds are that someone has at least a black eye, if not broken bones, on any given day.

But Gazzy really looked bad. They'd removed the man-of-war with gloved hands, dunked Gazzy in salt water, slathered him with goo, and given him a bunch of shots, and he still looked like he'd been dragged behind a chariot for a couple miles.

Of course, seeing the wings had freaked everyone out, but this was the U.S. military, and they got over it real fast. I mean, if they can deal with Area 51, they can handle anything, right? Including Total, who had left Akila back at the hut and come at Angel's request.

"He's going to sleep for about a day," the navy doctor said with a smile. "These stings really take it out of you."

I glanced at the wall clock. "We're getting on a sub in six hours."

"Oh, no," said the doctor. "He can't go anywhere. Trust me, he's going to feel terrible when he wakes up. There's no way he's getting on a submarine."

It's taken me a while, but I've learned not to pointlessly butt heads about dumb decisions that I don't have to follow anyway. It's been a real step of personal growth for me. So now, for instance, I didn't even argue with the doctor.

Instead, I got organized: I sent Fang and Iggy off to find food, got a debriefing from Angel about the adventures they'd had under water while they were *supposed to be tucked into bed,* and finally, finally, curled up in the hospital armchair with Nudge, while she told us all about being a real kid at school.

"It was awesome," Nudge admitted. "I loved it. In just a few days, I learned more than I'd learned from weeks of watching TV."

"That's good," I forced myself to say, and given my highly developed skills of deception, I even sounded very sincere. "And I'm glad to see you're still among the winged."

Nudge looked embarrassed. "Yeah. But anyway. I realized I just missed you guys so much. And I was too worried about your mom," she told me. "I had to be here to help, if I could."

I hugged her. "I'm so glad to have you back! Although you missed all the BS."

"Whaaat?"

The others filled her in while I checked on Gazzy and watched the clock. The doctor said the Gasman would sleep for a day, which I took to be about four hours in bird-kid time. Sure enough, along about four-thirty in the morning, he woke up.

It was time to head down to the dock—I wasn't going to risk missing the sub. It felt like a month ago that my mom had been kidnapped. Who knew what had happened by now?

"You good to go?" I asked Gazzy, fluffing his saltwater-sticky hair with my fingers.

He did a systems check, then nodded. "Yep. Feel like crap, but I'm okay."

"You look pretty tough with that face," I said admiringly, and he gave a pleased smile.

"Okay, troops, let's mobilize," I said. We were all a little punchy from lack of sleep, but I knew a couple cups of coffee would perk us right up.

"Whoa, hold it!" said a voice. It was the nice doctor, standing in the doorway, holding Gazzy's chart.

"Sorry," I said briskly. "We've got a sub to catch."

"He can't go anywhere!" The doctor looked appalled. "People stay in bed for days from a man-of-war sting!"

"We heal fast," Gazzy said modestly.

"We were hoping for a chance to study you some more," the doc admitted.

I sighed. "If I got a nickel every time I heard that... Okay, guys, let's go."

The doctor planted his feet, crossed his arms, and blocked the door to the hallway.

"I'm sorry. I can't let you leave."

"Uh-huh." I looked at Fang. In seconds he'd crossed the room, opened the casement window, and jumped out. Total jumped out after him. A nurse, passing by in the hallway, screamed and dropped an armful of files.

Gazzy was next. "Thanks for everything, doc," he said, then leaped lightly out. He dropped out of sight, but soon rose, working his wings powerfully, looking good.

Someone yelled, "There goes another one!" as I was

busy hustling Iggy and Nudge out the window. Finally, it was my turn, and I hopped up to the window ledge.

"Thanks again," I said politely. "But like I said, we've got a sub to catch." Then I let myself fall out the window, watching the ground rush up from six stories below.

I spread my wings and felt the air press against them as I soared with the flock. I loved that feeling, relished that freedom. The sky was still predawn dark, the wind fresh but not cool.

Finally, it was time.

I'm coming, Mom. I'm coming to rescue you.

47

HERE ARE TWO THINGS I hadn't thought about when I'd insisted that the navy lend us a sub for the rescue:

1) The flock and I are just about the most claustrophobic life-forms you'll ever meet; and
2) We would be trapped in a relatively small, airtight space with *the Gasman*.

Now I was on the dock, staring at the open hatch, with its narrow ladder leading straight down.

We'd spent a lot of time on the *Wendy K.*, the research boat in Antarctica. So we knew that boat interiors were small and compact. But I hadn't really thought about how much more compact a submarine would be.

The U.S.S. *Minnesota* was a really big submarine, by sub standards, but it was still smaller than, say, Disney World. Or a wide-open beach. Or a desert. Or, hey, the *entire freaking sky.*

"Um, Max, you gonna go?" Nudge asked. There were two officers waiting for us. The seconds were ticking by.

It looked like I'd be climbing into a huge coffin.

It felt like that too.

I could not be a total wuss in front of all these people. Especially the flock.

I flicked a glance at Fang, and his face showed me that he understood what I was feeling, but he knew that I knew that I just had to suck it up and get on the dang sub.

I felt a cold sweat break out on the back of my neck. My throat was closing. My chest felt tight. I had an image of me trapped on the sub, under water, crying and clawing at the metal walls to get out. Oh, geez. I was wishing I hadn't had that third espresso.

I swallowed hard and tried to draw in a breath. I remembered that we were doing this to rescue my mom, who had saved my own life more than once. I remembered that she was being held captive in a sub probably not half as nice as this one.

"It's a sub, Max," urged Total, who was suffering from a bad case of missing-Akila blues, "not a vat of boiling oil. Get on already, and let's see if they have any croissants. I'm starving."

I took a big step forward, off the dock and onto the metal

walkway that led to the top of the sub, not the sticking-up part of the sub, but the topside of its nose. I don't know the technical term.

There was an open hatch there, and I strode toward it, trying to keep abject terror from showing on my face. I began to climb down the ladder, managing a smile and a wave that I hoped was at least in the neighborhood of jaunty. Then Gazzy stepped on the walkway, followed by Total, and I knew the others weren't far behind.

There was no going back now.

Get this: if there was nothing inside the submarine, it might not be so bad. It really was a great big one. On the outside. On the inside, it was crammed chock-full of people, walls of instruments, panels of lights and switches, huge pipes and bundles of thick cables—basically, there was hardly any room to walk. And we're skinny.

There were not enough relaxation tapes in the world to get me through this.

Then Fang came up behind me and put his hand on my waist, just for a second. And I felt a little better.

The two officers zipped down the ladder, and one of them shouted the order to seal the hatch. Then he looked at us, these six weird, mostly tall, somewhat ungroomed children who had permission to be on a naval submarine. Plus their dog, who almost seemed like he could talk.

"Come with me," he said. "The birds are working again."

48

WALKING THROUGH the narrow corridors of the sub was like being inside someone's intestines, like we were making our way through the digestive tract. I kept expecting the Magic School Bus to show up and dump bile on us.

I absolutely refused to think about the fact that we were sealed inside this thing, sinking below the surface of the water. I kept repeating, *We're saving my mom,* over and over inside my head.

The officer stopped outside a door. All the doorways on a sub are shaped like Vienna Fingers cookies, kind of oblong. Each door has a sill about six inches high so that if the sub springs a leak and water gets in, each room can be sealed off. Oh, God, I was gonna die.

We stepped over the threshold and found ourselves in a small conference room. A tall man with short silver hair and dark brown eyes stood up and smiled. "I'm Captain Joshua Perry," he said, coming to shake hands with all of us. "I understand we have a mission to accomplish."

This wasn't what I was expecting.

Your mind creates your reality. If you expect nothing, you open up the universe to give you options. If you expect the worst, you usually get it.

The Voice. That really *was* the Voice, not my own thoughts and not something Angel was beaming into my brain. It was the Voice, loud and clear. And it had apparently been watching Oprah again.

Uh, Voice? Not that I'm not glad to hear you again, but this sub is already awfully crowded, and so is the inside of my head, so this might not be the best time...

"Max?" Captain Perry was looking at me.

"Sorry. What?"

"We haven't had any direct word about your mother. However, late last night, the following surveillance film was taken in the same general area as the first one that you saw. It looks strange because it was taken with a night-vision camera."

Someone dimmed the lights, and an image flickered on a white screen at one end of the room. It looked like daytime, except darker and kind of greenish. It was, like before, a huge expanse of featureless ocean. Covered with the shiny sides of dead, floating fish, as far as the eye could see. And attacking the seafood buffet were thousands of seabirds, who had clearly heard about the hundred-for-the-price-of-one special.

"We don't know what killed these fish," said the captain. "Several were recovered and tested. They were negative for traumatic injury, bacteria, parasites, starvation, fungal illnesses, cancers, enzyme imbalances, and gas bubble disease. They're simply dead, and we don't know why."

"Mass suicide?" Total muttered, clearly wishing he was back at the base with Akila.

"Then, look at this," said Captain Perry, pointing with a laser pen. The image pulled back; the camera was clearly attached to a rising helicopter. When the copter was quite high, it changed direction, as if heading back to land.

All of a sudden, in one tiny corner of the image, an enormous dark thing burst out of the water, sending dead fish flying everywhere and making the birds scatter. The camera quickly swung back to focus on it, and the helicopter started dropping altitude, but within moments the dark thing was gone without a trace.

"We've watched this film a hundred times now," said Captain Perry, "and we still can't tell what that was. It was almost like a mountain suddenly emerged from the ocean, then disappeared just as quickly. But sonar images show no large masses in that area whatsoever."

The lights flickered back on.

"What does this have to do with my mom?" I asked.

Captain Perry looked frustrated. "We don't know. In the earlier video, we saw part of the wrecked fishing boat in the background of the picture of Dr. Martinez being held hostage. This happened in the same area. The two instances of the dead fish, the enormous flock of birds, the huge thing rising out of the ocean—they're connected somehow. We just don't know how."

Everything is connected, Max, said the Voice. *Everything affects everything else, especially in the ocean.*

I gritted my teeth in frustration. I'd forgotten how incredibly annoying the Voice could be, with its fortune-cookie pronouncements.

"It's all got to be connected somehow," I said. "Are we headed there now?"

Captain Perry nodded. "We're keeping on code-red alert status, with full radar and sonar surveillance. We don't want that mountain to surge up and break *us* in half."

My eyes went wide. Was that even a possibility? Why hadn't someone told me this? Why was I even on this sub? If there's anything guaranteed to make me hyperventilate, it's being stuck in a place I can't punch my way out of.

It's okay, Max. I had to stop for a second and *distinguish* that this voice inside my head was Angel, not the Voice voice. *It's okay, Max,* Angel thought again. *If anything happens, we can all breathe under water, remember? It's like when we're on an airplane—if anything happens to it, we know six kids who will be fine. Same thing here. If anything happens to this sub, the six of us will be able to breathe through our gills. Trust me.*

Oh, *right*. Our *gills* would appear. Excellent. Now I felt better. *Not*.

49

THE MAN LOOKED at his second-in-command, who was looking at the third-in-command, who was staring accusingly at the fourth-in-command.

"They... escaped?" The man's voice was brusque.

The third-in-command kicked the fourth-in-command, who was kneeling on the floor, his forehead actually touching the cold metal.

"Yes, sir!" Everyone in the room knew the high cost of admitting such a thing. They also knew how much worse it would have been if he had lied about it. "I beg your forgiveness, sir! But they threw themselves over the edge of a cliff. Our trackers were programmed to follow them—no matter what. They kept attacking, sir. And they went over the cliff as well."

"But they couldn't fly, could they, Zhou Tso?"

"N-no, sir." He cringed.

"Unlike our quarry, who can."

"Yes, sir!"

Mr. Chu thought for a moment, though he already knew what he was going to do. The weakest link in the chain always had to be eliminated. The men and women he answered to would expect no less.

He again met the eyes of his second-in-command. The fourth had failed, which was a failure of the third, who had picked and trained him. So it was also the second's failure, since she had picked and trained the third. Ultimately, this was Chu's own failure, for he had picked and trained his second. That was how it would be viewed by the board. They all knew it.

Mr. Chu sighed, then motioned to his second-in-command. She gave a quick nod, then barked instructions at the two armed guards by the doorway. The fourth-in-command cringed and started to beg for mercy but was immediately silenced. The guards dragged him from the room.

Mr. Chu again sighed heavily. If only the girl had joined his force! It would have been glorious. Instead, she had turned into an increasingly intolerable problem. Fortunately, he was holding the final ace: her mother, Dr. Valencia Martinez.

Clasping his hands behind his back, Mr. Chu turned to look out the small, thick portholes in his office wall. He knew the fourth-in-command's solution would take several minutes. "Now the... mutants are on a U.S. Navy submarine?" Mr. Chu verified, gazing out at the blackness.

"Yes." There was a world of frustration in that one word.

Mr. Chu turned and met the eyes of his second-in-command. "Attacking a U.S. submarine, armed with nuclear warheads, would be suicide. Not only for us, but for those we represent. Even on a global level."

The second-in-command was torn but was forced to admit that Mr. Chu was right. "Yes." She let out the word.

"But, of course, if something were to happen to the bird people while they were not on the submarine..." Mr. Chu let his words trail off, and turned to stare out the portholes. At this depth, no light filtered down from the surface.

One of the armed guards dragged in Dr. Martinez. "Ah, Dr. Martinez," Mr. Chu said pleasantly. "Thank you for joining me. I wanted you to see this. If the CSM does not curtail its activity, a similar fate awaits you."

There was a slight vibration, and Mr. Chu's gaze sharpened. Then—there it was—a rush of bubbles, barely visible, from a torpedo hatch being opened and closed. It was the fourth-in-command's final solution. A dim, pale object in a blue suit shot out into the blackness and seemed to blossom, momentarily, in the dark water. In the next second, it was crushed and compressed into an unrecognizable blob.

At this depth, the water pressure was equivalent to several tons of weight per square inch.

The fourth-in-command had probably suffered for less than a second, not even having time to drown before every bone in his body was pulverized.

Once again, Mr. Chu and his second-in-command met eyes. "Well, outside the submarine, it's a very dangerous environment."

The second, not daring to display the shiver of distaste and fear she felt, nodded. "Yes," she said as the pale blob floated away into the dark water. "Yes, it's very dangerous out there."

50

I'LL BE THE FIRST to admit that in terms of book learning, we're right up there with, like, sheep and goats. So you won't be stunned to hear how surprised I was to find out that islands don't float on top of the water. You can't go under them, even if you're in a schmancy expensive submarine.

"Islands are formed several different ways," Brigid explained helpfully while I tried not to snarl at her. We were standing around a topographical (read: lumpy) map of Hawaii and the surrounding ocean. "Hawaii was formed by an underwater volcano spitting hot magma up from the earth's core. In fact, scientists believe that one volcano formed all the islands of Hawaii, as the hot interior core rotated beneath the earth's crust. Right now, the Big Island is being formed. In ten million years, there might be yet another island, past the Big Island."

"Huh," I said, feeling more trapped than ever. We'd been on the sub for eight hours and had explored every last inch of it. I felt like I hardly had room to breathe. It was like, *Hello, Claustrophia? It's me, Max.*

Now I was being forced to witness Dr. Amazing's brain at work, as Fang paid attention to her every word.

"Which is why we have to go around the islands to get to the area where the fish die-off was observed," said Captain Perry. "Right now we're passing the Molokini Crater, which is a big sea-life preservation area."

"Huh," I said. We were in a large tin can under six hundred feet of water, and I couldn't escape. I was starting to feel dizzy. Was the sub *running out of air*? Where did we *get* air from, anyway? We needed to *surface*. We needed to surface, and—

Max. Go lie down. You're having a panic attack.

What?! I thought wildly.

You're having a panic attack, the Voice went on. *Go lie down on your bunk and slowly breathe in and out.*

"Uh, I'm tired," I mumbled. "Think I'll go rest."

I stumbled out of the situation room and staggered down the narrow corridor, squeezing past sailors. I felt like I might pass out any second. Every cell in my body wanted to get off this sub. Even knowing that it was the only way to rescue my mom didn't make it any better. I've been locked in cells and dungeons and dog crates and never panicked like this.

You're okay, said the Voice soothingly. *Go lie down. There's plenty of air.*

I fumbled my way into the small storeroom that had been turned into our bunk room. Inside, I collapsed on one of the bottom bunks, trying not to throw up. A minute later, the door pushed open.

"Nudge?" I croaked, my hand over my mouth.

"Nope," said Total, trotting up to my bunk. He had a cold, wet washcloth in his mouth, and he put his front paws on my bunk and dropped it on my face. It felt incredible. Then he nimbly jumped onto the narrow bunk and curled up by my feet.

I pressed the wet cloth to my face and tried to breathe in and out slowly. Just like the Voice had told me. I moaned softly, suddenly overwhelmed by my life.

"You'll get your sea legs soon," Total said. "Or we can rustle you up some Valium or something."

"No!" The only time I'd had Valium was when my mom gave me some during an operation to take a chip out of my wrist (long story). In my hazy stupor, I'd said all sorts of stupid, embarrassing things. There was *no way* I was going to do that again.

"Suit yourself," said Total, pushing my legs over to give himself more room. "Listen, Max, while I have you here—"

"Trapped in my bunk with a panic attack?" I said.

"Yeah. Anyway, I've been meaning to talk to you," he went on.

Oh, this was gonna be good. What would it be now? Sub chow not up to snuff? Lattes not available? Had he encountered more discrimination against Canine Americans?

"It's about Akila."

I lowered the washcloth and peeked at Total with one eye. "Yeah? You miss her, huh?"

"It's more than that." Total licked one paw, collecting his thoughts. "It's—you know I'm nuts about her."

"Uh-huh." *Nuts* being the operative word here.

"Amazingly, she feels the same way about a mutt like me," Total said. "Well, now we're thinking about... marriage." He sort of mumbled the last word.

I sat up, eyes wide, swallowing my shocked laughter. This wasn't funny. It was cute but not funny. Total's feelings were real, even though he was a—Canine American.

"Marriage?" I said.

"Yeah." Total flopped down and draped his head over my ankles. "I know we're just two crazy kids—how can we possibly make it work? She's a dedicated career dog. How could I ever expect her to settle down, raise a few litters? And me? I'm a flying, talking dog. I'll only make her life more difficult, no matter where we go or what we do."

I knew how he felt. Only too well. Reaching out, I scratched his head between his ears, the way he likes.

"Also, how could I ever leave you guys?" he said, his

black eyes sad. "I know how much you depend on me. How could I leave you to fend for yourselves?"

"Um," I said, but he interrupted me.

"But Akila can't fly! How can *she* come with *us*? She's eighty pounds of gorgeous, long-legged purebred, but she can't fly." His voice broke. "I tell you, Max—this has been keeping me up at night. I haven't been able to eat for days."

I'd heard him snoring just yesterday, when we'd been waiting for the sub, and I've never known him to miss a meal. But I knew what he meant.

For once, I didn't have any answers. I was having a hard enough time with my own ridiculous romantic life, much less being able to worry about anyone else's. "Total—if you decide you need to stay with Akila—well, you saw how Nudge made that hard decision. I saw something written on a T-shirt once—it went: 'If you love something, let it go. If it comes back, it's yours.' If we, the flock, have to let you go, we'll somehow make that sacrifice."

"No, no, Max, I couldn't ask that of you," he said. "I wouldn't leave you in the lurch like that. I just wish—well, I wish life was perfect and love was easy." He sighed.

"Me too, Total. Me too." I was already old enough to know that neither option was possible. Not for Total and not for me.

51

IT TOOK TWELVE HOURS to go a distance that we could have flown in about six minutes. Let's stop for a second and give thanks that the mad scientists decided to graft us with *bird* DNA instead of, say, the DNA of a clam or a squid.

Our sub went between the islands of Maui and Hawaii and then surfaced, right offshore from the Haleakala National Park. Of course, as soon as I heard the sub-wide command of "Surfacing!" I dashed up to the ladder that led to the upper hatch. I was the second one out, gulping in lungfuls of fresh, balmy salt air.

I turned to Captain Perry, who had joined me up on deck, along with John Abate and Brigid Dwyer. "So how come we're here?" I asked him.

"We're picking up a marine biologist," Captain Perry explained.

"A colleague of ours," said John. "She specializes in bony fish, which are mostly what the dead groups have consisted of. Ah, here she comes now."

A short, tan woman with gray hair in a long braid came hurrying down the dock. In the distance, I could a bunch of kids, who'd just disembarked from a school bus with FREMONT MIDDLE SCHOOL on the side, gaping at the nuclear sub that had suddenly surfaced so near the entrance to a national park.

"Hello!" the woman called cheerfully. "Aloha!"

"Aloha," said Captain Perry respectfully.

"Noelani! It's good to see you again," said John, giving her a hug. He turned to me. "Max, this is Doctor Noelani Akana. She knows these waters like you know junk food, and she can help us."

"Hi," I said, deciding whether to be offended by the junk-food comment.

"Ah, Max," she said, in a pretty, singsong voice. I guessed she was a native Hawaiian. Her bright, black eyes looked me over shrewdly but not in an unfriendly way. "Max, the miracle bird girl."

"Uh, that's one name for me," I said awkwardly.

Dr. Akana broke into a sunny smile. "I can't wait to see the others! All right, Captain, let's get this ship under water!" With quick, efficient movements, she tossed her duffel bag down the hatch, then slid down the ladder rails.

John, grinning, followed her. Captain Perry looked at me and motioned at the hatch.

"How about I just fly overhead and meet you there?" I said.

"Okay," the captain said easily, surprising me. "How long can you hover without landing on anything?"

"Uh, I guess about eight hours," I said, knowing it would be a stretch and that I'd be totally starving and exhausted by the end of it.

Captain Perry waited.

"Okay, fine," I said, heading toward the hatch. I *hate* it when a grown-up actually calls my bluff. Of course, this was pretty much the first time, so I don't have to deal with it too often.

"You know, we can get you some Valium or something," he offered, following me.

"No!" I gritted my teeth and began to climb down the ladder. "Why does everyone keep wanting to drug a *child?*"

Dr. Akana was waiting at the bottom of the ladder, and she clapped her hands as if organizing a party game. "Okay! We're going closer to where the attacks took place, then stop at about sixty meters deep. Then we'll go on a field trip. Let me put my stuff down, and I'll get ready." She headed off to the quarters she'd share with the female crew members.

I felt a surge of excitement. *At last,* we were on our way. I had to get into battle mode, make sure the others were ready for the traditional fight-to-the-death scenario. The navy wanted to make sure we could defend ourselves, but they'd never really seen us in action.

For the first time ever, I wondered if we had what it would take—Mr. Chu and his dumb-bots I was pretty sure we could handle. But sea monsters? Mountains that came out of the water to kill a hundred thousand fish? That was a completely different picture. I needed a plan B.

Frowning, I made my way into the belly of the ship to find Gazzy.

52

"THERE'S ONLY ROOM for three," I told Angel, who was getting that mutinous look on her face.

"I should go, because I might hear something," she said, crossing her arms over her chest.

By "hear," I knew she meant telepathically pick up on something, like the fish thinking little bubbly fish thoughts ("Ooh! Plankton!") or whatever. "It's too dangerous," I said firmly, which was pretty much the lamest argument I could have come up with, given the sheer amount of completely death-defying stuff we did on a routine basis.

"Max." She looked at me, and I remembered that she could also put thoughts *into* people's heads.

"Don't make me wish I was wearing a foil hat," I warned her. "Look, the crewman has to go, because he knows how to drive the little sub, and Dr. Akana has to go because she knows what the heck we'll be looking at, and I have to go because (a) I'm the leader, right? And (b) it's my mom we're looking for, and (c) because I said so. You dig?"

I crossed my arms too and frowned down at her, something that's always worked in the past, but I doubted it would for much longer.

"Angel, dear, you're only six," Dr. Akana said kindly.

"Seven," Angel said obstinately.

"When did you turn seven? Oh, never mind," I said, getting exasperated. None of us knows when our actual birthdays are, so we each made up one for ourselves. Years ago I'd had to put my foot down about getting only one birthday a year, because Gazzy was trying to capitalize on presents. But, actually, we don't really keep track of them too well.

"I'm seven." Angel looked like a bulldozer wouldn't budge her.

"Fine, then, I'm—seventeen!" I said. "You're not going."

The little sub in question was a three-person thingy that looked kind of like a large pool float with a bubble on top. It could go down to one hundred meters (about three hundred feet—our Big Daddy sub could go down about one thousand meters), and I practically expected to see foot pedals sticking out the bottom.

The only reason I was willing to get in it was because of the Plexiglas dome on top that you could see out of. Our current sub had *no windows.* I repeat, *no windows.* Zero. Zip. *Nada.* That was because the space between the outer hull and the inner hull was full of water when the sub submerged and full of air when it surfaced. A window would have had to have been about a foot thick. Instead, the crew viewed the outside on little TV screens, from cameras located on the sub's exterior.

But now I had a chance to be in a big bubble and see what was going on. Anything would be better than being stuck in here.

I rubbed my hands together. "Let's do it."

Ten minutes later, a bottom hatch slowly opened, and we dropped down into the deep ocean. There wasn't much light, but because the water around Hawaii is so clear, it wasn't totally pitch dark, even at sixty meters deep.

Then the crewman turned on the headlights. It was amazing—our own underwater show. Above us was the enormous U.S.S. *Minnesota.* We were chugging out from under it, thank God. But the fish! There were fish everywhere, all sizes, moving slowly through the water.

"That's a yellowfin tuna," said Dr. Akana. "They can grow to more than seven feet long."

"What's that one?!" I said, pointing to a huge silver hubcap with orange fins.

"It's an opah," said the crewman. "They're good eatin.'"

"It's almost as big as me," I said.

"I'm sure it weighs more," Dr. Akana said with a smile. "Look! There's a turtle!"

Sure enough, a turtle about the size of a standard poodle swam by, looking totally unconcerned about our sub.

"Everything moves so slowly under water," I said. In addition to the fish that caught our attention because they were the size of sofas, we were surrounded by hundreds of thousands of smaller fish in every shape and color combination you could imagine—and some you couldn't.

"Not everything—these fish can dart away in an instant if danger's near," said Dr. Akana. "Now, we're still about six miles away from where the fish kill was first spotted, but I wanted to check out—" Her words were swallowed by a gasp. "Oh, my God! What's that!?"

My head whipped to where she was staring, and I sucked in a fast breath.

No, I thought. *Not this*.

53

"CONTACT THE SUB!" Dr. Akana commanded the crewman urgently. "Issue a Mayday!"

"Hang on," I said, still staring out the Plexiglas dome. Thirty feet away, and swimming closer to us, was something I never expected to see but should have.

"Contact the sub!" the doctor cried.

"Nah, don't bother," I said, narrowing my eyes. "I'll deal with her myself."

"Max! She's drowning!"

"She's *swimming*," I corrected her. "And being obnoxious. And getting into major trouble." I frowned at Angel, who was maybe ten feet away now, smiling and waving at us. *You are in deep sneakers,* I thought hard at her, and her smile faltered.

Then she grinned again, swimming loop-de-loops in front of us.

"She has no gear," said Dr. Akana weakly. "She'll run out of air."

"She has gills," I admitted, still glaring at Angel. Sure, she didn't have to worry about air, but there were a million other dangerous things in the ocean, including some huge, catastrophic mystery that might have something to do with my mom being kidnapped. And here Angel was, swimming around like she was bulletproof and sharkproof and man-of-war proof!

"Gi—"

"Gills," I repeated, as Angel merrily caught a ride on a manta ray the size of a mattress. "We've all got other special skills and stuff. Angel can breathe under water. Also, she can communicate with fish and read people's thoughts. Don't play poker with her."

The crewman swore softly under his breath. "She took me for forty bucks!"

Angel came back and clung to our clear dome. While I gave her every fierce look in my repertoire, she pressed her mouth against the Plexiglas and blew her cheeks out. Then she pulled off and laughed hard, doubling over and emitting a stream of bubbles.

"Is she not affected by water pressure?" Dr. Akana asked. "We're sixty meters deep! A scuba diver would have to be very cautious about getting the bends."

"She'll get the bends all right," I muttered. "I'm gonna bend her over my knee!"

Staying in our headlights, Angel performed an underwater ballet, first following a turtle, then another ray, then a mahimahi. She imitated their swimming styles, embellishing them with flourishes, spins, and somersaults. She kept her wings tight against her back, as we all did when we swam. She was having a super time. I was going to kill her.

"Besides the swimming child with gills, I'm not seeing anything unusual here," said Dr. Akana humorously. "The marine life looks healthy and undisturbed. I see no evidence of algae blooms or coral reef die-off. I don't see huge amounts of dead fish."

"But we're still far away, right?" I asked.

"Yes. I thought we should start taking stock of things this far away and continue to check periodically as we get closer to the site," she explained.

I jumped as Angel tapped on the dome above my head. While I scowled at her, she pointed to me, to my neck, and then out to the water.

"What is she saying?" asked Dr. Akana.

"She wants me out there, to see if I've developed gills," I said, and only after I saw the crewman's eyes widen did I realize how nuts that sounded. Well, I already had wings, air sacs in addition to lungs, and was almost five-eight but weighed barely more than a hundred pounds. If this guy was looking for normal, I ain't it.

"Do things just develop like that on you?" Dr. Akana sounded fascinated. How scientisty of her.

I nodded. "I mean, not all the time, you know," I said, feeling embarrassed by the crewman, who was obviously trying not to look shocked. "But every so often, something new happens or changes on one or more of us. Like we were programmed to keep evolving."

"That is so amazing," said Dr. Akana softly. "You are truly special and unique, Max."

I felt my cheeks grow warm, as the "circus sideshow freak" factor rose by the second.

A quick movement caught our eyes. I swiveled to see an enormous shark making its way toward us. Its tail was slicing back and forth, its head wagging as if looking for prey.

"Uh-oh," said the crewman. "You better get that little girl out of there."

"Yeah." *Angel? Big shark alert.* I thought hard. I can't actually send my own thoughts, but Angel usually monitors stuff going on around her.

We watched as she paused in midpirouette to look for the shark. They spotted each other at the same time. The shark took only a second to sum up Angel as being snackworthy and immediately began a fast, efficient approach.

"Crewman!" said Dr. Akana. "Put the *Triton* between Angel and the shark!"

The crewman immediately began to maneuver our small vehicle, even as he said, "Not sure the *Triton* can withstand an attack from a shark that size, ma'am."

Angel faced the shark, looking at it intently. She held up one hand as Dr. Akana winced, bracing for the worst. I sat frozen.

The shark paused. Angel swam up to it. I heard the crewman suck in a breath, heard Dr. Akana praying softly. The shark stayed still, and Angel ran her hand gently along its head. It rubbed against her like a huge, toothy dog. Angel turned to grin at us.

"Okay, folks. Show's over," I said. "Let's get back to the *Minnesota*."

54

"YOU'VE GOT TO QUIT just thinking about yourself!" I said as Angel stuck out her bottom lip and crossed her arms over her chest.

And you've got to start paying more attention to her, said the Voice. *And to what she's saying.*

"Oh, like I don't already?" I snapped aloud, then saw Angel's look of confusion. I shook my head. "Never mind. But I was worried sick while you were out there!"

"You're worrying about the wrong things, Max," said Angel. "You should be trying to breathe under water and taking care of yourself. You don't have to worry about me."

"It's my job to worry about you!" I said, shocked. "It always has been!" Angel had been about two years old when Jeb kidnapped us from the School. He hadn't known what to do with her. Guess who took care of her night and day? And every day since then? Right. *Moi*.

Angel looked sad. "We're family, Max. I'm not a job."

"That's not what I mean, and you know it," I said.

"Okay, let's break it up," said Fang from behind me, making me jump. I hadn't heard him come in, as usual. "Angel, you're still a little kid, and Max is the leader. Don't forget that."

Angel looked chastised. "Well, I'm going to go get into some dry clothes. Come on, Total. Let me tell you about everything I saw out there."

"Could we talk about something else?" said Total, as he trotted after her, jumping over the door's threshold. "Like, modern art? Or my latest issue of *Wine Spectator* magazine? Fish and me—we don't mix. It really seems more like a feline thing."

I watched them go, thinking for the millionth time that things had been so much easier when it had been just the six of us, on our own.

"You handled that really well, Fang," said—you guessed it—Brigid. I tried not to gag as she patted his arm approvingly. Fang shot me a smug look over her shoulder, knowing it would make my blood pressure rise. I thought about the last time he'd made my blood pressure rise (in a completely different way) and felt a warm flush stain my cheeks.

I looked at Fang. "Can we have a meeting? With the flock?"

He nodded.

"That's a good idea," Brigid said. "I'd like to ask you—"

"This is flock business," I said abruptly.

Brigid looked taken aback. "But we're all a team."

"Yes," I said. "And I really, really appreciate everyone's help in finding my mom. But some things are still just for the flock. It's always been that way, and it'll always be that way. 'Cause when it comes right down to it, there's us six, and no one else is like we are."

Disappointed, Brigid nodded. Fang and I headed down to our little bunk room. We opened the door and found a typical scene: Angel and Total were curled up on a bunk (the sailors called them "racks"), looking at Total's issue of *Wine Spectator.* Nudge had deconstructed her small khaki uniform and was holding a needle and thread as she turned it into something that didn't offend her fashion sensibilities.

As soon as I walked in, Gazzy stuffed something behind a pillow, and Iggy put on his oh-so-obvious "innocent" face, which immediately set off all alarms.

"Max!" said Nudge happily. "Look! I took off the collar and changed the neckline. Once I move the buttons, it'll be so much cuter."

I wanted to say, "It'll still be khaki," but didn't want to rain on her fashion parade. My eyes were riveted on telltale wires sticking out from beneath Gazzy's pillow.

"Gazzy, I swear to God, if you've stolen a nuclear device, I will—"

"It's not nuclear!" he insisted.

I sat down on the lowest narrow rack and pushed my hair out of my face, trying to figure out what to say. I am excellent at giving orders and barking out commands. I am not so good with the touchy-feely, "let's connect" kind of stuff. But a leader has to press on sometimes, even with things she doesn't like. It's all part of the leaderly gig.

"Guys," I began gently. So far, so good. "I feel like we've gotten off track."

"What do you mean, Max?" Nudge's eyes were wide.

"We've been hanging with the navy for days now, and we're not any closer to rescuing my mom. It made sense to hook up with them, at first, but now I wonder if they have any real plans. I'm thinking—well, I'm thinking that I want to give them another twelve hours. And if we haven't made real progress, if we're not any closer to rescuing my mom, then I think we should ditch 'em and head out on our own."

Six pairs of eyes looked at me. Did they still trust me? Did they want to follow what the grown-ups said? Was I going to be in this all by myself?

My throat felt tight as I waited.

Then Fang put out his right fist. Nudge put hers on top, quickly. Then Gazzy, Angel, Iggy, and finally, Total put his paw at the top.

"One for all and all for one," said Fang, as my heart filled up. "That was in some movie."

I put my fist on top of Total's paw, my smile so wide my cheeks ached.

"Thanks, guys," I said. "Now, let's see if we can get this show on the road."

And of course it was at that very moment that we felt a huge *crunch* and were jolted so hard we fell off our racks, and the lights went out.

55

QUICK RECAP: claustrophobic, paranoid bird kid, trapped on jam-packed navy tin can of death, submerged under hundreds of feet of water, and now, huge crashing sound and no lights.

Okay, have you got that picture? Now ramp up the adrenaline about 400 percent. Mix in a little terror. Stir.

"That didn't sound good," I said, trying to be the calm, confident leader I am, even though every cell in my body was shrieking that I was about to die a horrible, watery death.

Emergency lights flickered on and glowed a dim amber. A Klaxon alarm sounded, just like in all the old submarine movies. That's the one you hear right before the sub goes belly-up.

Because metal and water conduct sound well, we could hear pounding and knocking against the hull of the sub. I opened the door and saw sailors rushing past, each knowing what their job was, where they had to be.

"I wish we were in France." Total whimpered softly.

Out in the corridor, the alarm was louder.

The most horrible thing about this whole experience was that I didn't know what to do. I *always* know what to do. I am chock-full of knowingness. Every awful thing we've come up against until now, I've been able to deal with. A mixture of ruthless cunning, wicked fighting skills, and sheer stoic toughness had gotten us this far. But none of that seemed to be worth much in this situation.

To save face, I started barking orders anyway. "Let's go up front, by the main hatch," I commanded, oozing confidence. "If we have to abandon ship, that's where we'll escape from."

We waited for a break in the line of running sailors, then threw ourselves into the passageway and started rushing forward. It seemed to take forever, with us hurrying and jumping over all the raised thresholds. Around us, sailors were sealing off compartments with their little turny-wheel things.

All of a sudden Angel stopped dead, causing the rest of us to pile into her.

"Angel, go!" I yelled.

"No, wait!" she said, holding up her hand.

"We can't wait! We need to get up front! Move it!"

"Wait," she insisted. "It's the dumb-bots."

"Whaat?"

"It's those M-Geeks, the dumb-bots," Angel said. "They're trying to get into the sub."

Lovely, just lovely. I'll fight anything on the surface or in the air, but under water? I was *literally* out of my element, so much more than anyone else is who *says* they're out of their element, like at a party. I pictured the M-Geeks drilling through the sub walls, pictured it filling up with water, with us trapped inside...

"Okay," I said firmly. "We need to stop them. I'll get the *Triton*."

"Does it have weapons?" Iggy asked.

"No. But it has big claw arms," I said. "Maybe I can whack them or knock them off or something."

"Here, take this," Gazzy said, pushing a small metal first-aid box into my hands. "It's waterproof, so put it in the claw. And here's a remote. Don't sit on it or anything. Push the button to watch a DVD, then use the *Triton*'s claw to toss it at the M-Geeks. Do it fast."

"Okay. You guys go forward," I said. "I'll catch up soon."

"I'm going with you," said Fang.

I looked at him. "I need you to take care of the others," I said very quietly. After a conflicted moment, he nodded.

"I'll go with you," said Gazzy. "I know how to work the IED."

I hated to let him, but he was right. "Okay."

"I'm going too," said Angel.

"No, Angel, please," I said, trying not to beg. "Please stay with Fang."

"I want to go too." There was that face again.

"Angel, come with me," Fang said, taking her hand. "Iggy, Nudge, let's move it." He headed quickly down the hall, all but dragging Angel with him.

I watched them go down the dark narrow corridor, hoping it wasn't the last time I'd ever see them. I turned to Gazzy and handed him the metal box. "Let's go. We've got a *Triton* to steal and dumb-bots to kill."

56

I'VE HOT-WIRED quite a few cars and driven all kinds of weird vehicles, like a school bus and a tank. Here are a couple of tips: school buses do not corner well, and tanks smell like old gym socks. I'd never stolen a *Triton,* but I had watched the crewman steer it around, and I thought I could do it. No one even tried to stop Gazzy and me as we raced back down the corridor and entered the pressure chamber.

The *Triton* was sitting there waiting for us.

"So cool!" Gazzy said. "Did you jack a key?"

I grinned. "No key. Just a push button."

Gazzy took his metal box and put it on the floor right next to one of the *Triton*'s arms, then we scrambled up to the dome and opened the hatch. We dropped down into the seats, and I started flicking switches, hoping I was doing it in the right order. I'd only seen it done once. Gazzy sealed the hatch, and all the panels lit up inside. He looked thrilled, but I wasn't any happier about this than I was the first time.

Then it hit me, amid all the flashing lights and alarms and the banging sounds that were getting louder: a realization that made my blood run cold and my hand freeze into a claw on the single joystick that operated the sub.

I was locked in a very small airtight container... with *the Gasman.*

I'm not huge with religion, but right then I started praying to every deity I'd ever heard of. *Please do not let Gazzy have one of his episodes in here. Please.*

The Voice suddenly chimed in: *Get a move on, Max.*

Right, right. Inside the sub, I grabbed the remote that would open the chamber doors, dropping us out into the ocean.

"Gaz, you have the arm operators right there," I said, pointing. Dr. Akana had used them to gather small samples of water. "Pick up your metal box."

Gazzy caught on to the simple hand controls and quickly swept up the box with the claw. Then I hit my remote. Suddenly the doors beneath us opened, and the *Triton* slid clumsily into the ocean as I tried to keep us level.

It was way dark, and I peered out through the Plexiglas bubble, not wanting to turn on the headlights. Stealth was the answer here, and we would be as stealthy as a bright yellow, three-ton, bubble-trailing baby sub could be.

"I can't tell where the noise is coming from," said Gazzy. "We'll have to check the whole sub."

I nodded, jerkily moving us forward.

"Maybe I should drive," Gazzy offered.

"Shut up," I said, concentrating. We started sinking fast, and I frantically worked the lever to make us rise up and stabilize. I hated this. I hated it with a whole new kind of hate that I should probably have reserved for Mr. Chu.

Sweat broke out on my forehead, and my hand started cramping up from clutching the joystick too tightly. But I got us out from under the *Minnesota,* and we started trailing along its side toward the back.

Gazzy practiced maneuvering the arms, and he accidentally whacked a big grouper in the side of its head. It darted off, while he muttered, "Sorry, sorry!"

"Do you see anything?" I asked.

"You mean, besides the sub the size of a football stadium? And a bunch of fish? Nope."

I was getting better at driving, and we putt-putted alongside the sub. What was going on in there? Had the others made it to the front? Were they getting ready to evacuate?

Tap, tap! I almost screamed when something knocked on the Plexiglas above our heads. If the dumb-bots got a hold of the *Triton*...

Angel's smiling face looked down at us. My eyes almost popped out of my head. She had done this *again,* after I'd lectured her the first time! I started yelling at her, but she ignored me, instead urgently pointing toward the aft of the *Minnesota*.

I pushed the joystick forward and in another couple seconds, saw what she was warning me about: eight M-Geeks, clinging to the side of the big sub. One was wielding an underwater welding torch, and it was attempting to cut through the sub's hull.

"Angel! Get behind us! Hide!" I yelled as loud as I could, which *of course* caused her to immediately let go of us and swim directly *toward* the M-Geeks.

I flicked on the headlights and again shoved the joystick forward, trying to increase our speed. I was forming a vague plan of having one of the *Triton*'s arms grab Angel somehow, but in another two seconds Angel had gotten close enough to the M-Geeks to actually tap on one's head.

Immediately, all of them stopped working and swiveled to look at her. In the next instant, they had quickly grouped around her, and I saw they had little motors keeping them stable in the water.

"Do you see her?" I asked Gazzy tensely.

"Uh-uh." His voice sounded choked. "They're surrounding her. And I can't use my bomb."

I moved forward cautiously. The eight M-Geeks were a cluster of metal, tools, and weapons, shining brightly in my headlights. And there was no sign of Angel anywhere.

57

"I'M GONNA RAM them," I said.

"No—you might crush her!"

"Okay, I'm gonna start batting them out of the way then," I said, edging the *Triton* closer.

"Max, be careful!"

"What else can I do?" I exclaimed. "I don't exactly want to open our hatch and see if I've developed gills yet! We've got to get Angel out of there!"

Every muscle in my body was as taut as a wire as I moved closer to the throng of M-Geeks. Somewhere in that mess of violent metal was my baby, my Angel. She might think she could rule the world and do anything, but I knew that despite all her powers, she was still a flesh-and-blood, six-(possibly seven)-year-old girl. Who I needed to save. Again.

"Okay, you work the arms," I whispered. "Try to push one aside."

Gazzy's face was white as he nodded, his hands clenched on the controls.

"On my mark," I said. "One, two, thr—"

Suddenly the dumb-bots moved apart, revealing Angel. She seemed to be talking to them earnestly, motioning with her hands, trailing tiny bubbles out of her mouth.

I stared at her, then at Gazzy, whose jaw had dropped in surprise.

Then, as we watched, the dumb-bots seemed to huddle in for a consultation. A minute later, they started to disperse, heading off into the dark water one by one, their little fanlike rotors leaving small white trails behind them. Angel waved good-bye to them, then turned and wiggled her eyebrows at me and Gazzy.

I gave her the universal WTH expression, and she grinned and dog-paddled closer to the *Triton*. Clinging to the side, she went through an elaborate "told you so" pantomime.

With Angel still holding on, I turned the *Triton* around and headed back to the *Minnesota*, feeling overwhelming relief, tension, and extreme irritation all at the same time.

I was giving Angel a look of "Wait till we get back on board, missy," which she was cheerfully ignoring, when her face suddenly went blank. Then her eyes widened in fear, and she pressed herself flat against the Plexiglas dome, her small knuckles white.

"What? *What?*" I cried. She looked in at me, and my heart turned to ice when I saw how scared she was.

In the next moment, a powerful swell of water came out of nowhere and swept us beneath the bigger sub, making us crash against its underside. Angel clung to the *Triton* and hunkered down.

"What the—there aren't currents like this, this deep!" I said. Our dome smashed against the metal sub again, and my throat closed as I wondered just how tough the Plexiglas was.

"Holy crap!" Gazzy shouted, pointing.

A mountain was coming up out of the murky depths below us, creating such a huge swell that the *Minnesota* was actually tipping to one side. We crashed against the sub again, and I jammed the joystick forward, desperately trying to get back to the underwater hatch we had exited from.

"What the heck is that thing?" I cried. If I couldn't keep us angled right, Angel would be smashed between us and the sub. I yanked the joystick to the left.

Off to one side, the mountainous thing moved past us, heading toward the surface. I saw now that it had a beginning and an end and wasn't quite Everest-sized but still totally qualified as ginormously freaking big.

"There!" Gazzy pointed above us, and punched the remote that opened the *Minnesota*'s bottom hatch. The next water swell carried us up into the belly of the sub, Angel still holding on tightly.

"Close the hatch!" I commanded. The hatch doors closed beneath us, and lights flashed as the hydraulic pumps began to force water out of the chamber. Another twenty seconds, and we popped the *Triton*'s hatch, breathing in the damp air. Gazzy and I quickly jumped out, and I grabbed Angel, who was sopping wet and shivering. Holding her tightly, I stroked her hair.

"What happened with the M-Geeks?" I asked.

"I just asked them to go away," she said. "They said okay."

"O-kaaaay," I said. "And what was the swimming mountain?"

Big troubled eyes met mine. "I don't know, Max. It's like nothing I've ever felt before—not like a person or an alien or a mutant. But—it was *thinking*. It has thoughts. It's intelligent. And it wanted to kill. It wanted to kill everything."

Just then something hit the sub hard, knocking us off balance. More alarms blared, and we heard shouting. There was a gut-wrenching grinding, the sound of screeching metal, then the sub went silent, tilted on its side.

We were dead in the water.

58

BITTER IRONY crushed me: we'd escaped death so many times on land and in the air, only to be doomed to die in the ocean.

I'd read news reports about a hundred Russian sailors who had all died trapped in their sub in less than two hundred feet of water. We were in much worse shape. I didn't know if the sea monster would be back, or if the M-Geeks had really gone away. I didn't know if we were sinking slowly into the darker, colder depths of the ocean, never to rise again. With the power gone, we couldn't even limp back to the base. And at this depth, the water pressure was so great that the hatches couldn't be opened. There was no way out.

But a leader can't dwell on stuff like that. A leader has to lead.

"Okay, guys," I said, channeling confidence and authority. "First, let's get—"

The chamber door opened, and Total peeped in, the flashing red emergency lights highlighting his fur every couple seconds

"Yo," he said. "Sub's in trouble. Climb out here—we're doing an emergency surface."

"An emergency surface?" Quickly we scrambled up the slanted floor to the open doorway. Fang was standing behind Total, followed by Nudge and Iggy. My flock was together, and they'd come to find us.

"Yeah," said Fang, giving Gazzy a hand up. "There's all sorts of backup systems. Apparently. We're dumping ballast and pumping in air and should be at the surface in about half an hour."

Well. Let's hear it for those thoughtful sub designers, eh?

We ended up feeling our way to the front of the sub and were among the first off when it finally reached the surface. They popped the hatch and deployed inflatable life rafts. I've never been so thankful to breathe fresh air.

We bobbed around in the ocean in six-foot waves until navy choppers came. They lowered a long rope ladder, and some Navy SEALs jumped down into the water to help. It was all very controlled and orderly, which is, I gather, how the navy likes it.

"Children first!" shouted a SEAL, holding the ladder. "Let's go!"

There were eighteen sailors with us in our raft, all waiting for us to go first.

"Can we just meet you guys somewhere?" I asked John Abate. "We don't need to take up space in a chopper." *Plus I'm dying to stretch my wings and get up in the fresh air, where I feel normal.*

John nodded and quickly gave me directions to a marine research station about thirty miles away, where we'd meet.

I clapped once to get the flock's attention. "Okay, guys," I said. "Ready to do an up and away?"

They cheered and stood up.

"Please get on the ladder!" the SEAL barked.

"We're not getting on the ladder," I said firmly. "Thanks anyway. I really think you're being all you can be. But we're out of here."

It was hard to jump up into the air from an inflatable raft, but we managed, though we sank about a foot into the water before we were aloft. But finally there we were: moving our wings strongly, feeling the air blowing against our faces, our hair streaming back. It was heaven.

Below us, stunned sailors and crewmen stared up at what they'd heard about but had never expected to see. John and Brigid waved, and maybe I'm imagining things, but I thought Brigid looked envious. Maybe she wanted wings too.

"Thank God!" I said, climbing high above the ocean.

We soared until the rafts were tiny dots on the dark, gray blue water.

Angel was peering downward. "I'm trying to see that big thing," she said. "The big sea-monster thing."

We looked, and though we could make out whales and rays and sharks, nothing we saw looked anything like the moving mountain that had almost capsized our sub.

"Our new mission: figure out what that was," I said, as we turned in a lazy, thirty-degree arc back toward the big island of Hawaii. "I just know it has something to do with my mom—and Mr. Chu."

As we headed toward land and the marine research station where we'd meet up with the others, I had another, more disturbing thought: What exactly had Angel told the M-Geeks under water? Why hadn't they attacked her? They were machines, and I didn't think she could influence machines the way she could humans.

Did Angel know something about Mr. Chu I didn't?

59

THE MARINE RESEARCH STATION was kind of like the research station in Antarctica, but with no snow, carnivorous man-killing leopard seals, or Angel falling into deadly icy crevasses. Part of it was built out over the water, and there was a section of glass floor where you could look down and see fish and manta rays and sharks swimming beneath you.

The flock and I were lying flat on the glass to watch the fish, thankful that we were back on dry land again and not on a freaking sub.

An intern came to get us. "Will you join us in the conference room?"

I got to my feet. "Sure. I love conference rooms. Some

of the best times in my life have been in conference rooms. Can't get enough of 'em."

The intern looked at me oddly, but we followed him down the hall. Fang brushed up against me, and it reminded me that we hadn't had any time together, just the two of us, in days. Not that I wanted any. I just noticed is all.

The conference room held the usual cast of characters: John, Brigid, Dr. Akana, some navy types, some other scientisty-looking people who couldn't keep their eyes off us. I was used to crazed scientists in white lab coats coming at us with needles and electrodes and wrist restraints. I wasn't used to scientists who found us fascinating but still kept a respectful distance and treated us like we had actual rights and dignity and stuff. I mean, what was up with that?

"I've been developing a theory," said Brigid, walking to the front of the room. I sat down and tried not to glower at her, but I braced myself: maybe Brigid wanted to do a special mission, just her and Fang. The cow eyes she kept flashing at him made me want to drop-kick her to the middle of next week.

Brigid addressed us earnestly. "Since mankind first began venturing out to sea, there have been tales of sea monsters. Reading these old stories nowadays, we recognize that some of what they saw were regular whales or whale sharks or giant squid."

"What about the Loch Ness Monster?" Gazzy asked. He loved stuff like this.

"That's a myth," someone said.

"It's never been proved or disproved," Dr. Akana said. "Some people think Nessie is the last surviving plesiosaur. Some people think it's a mythical creature come to life, like a phoenix. And some people think it's always been a hoax."

"What we're dealing with now is not a hoax or a left-over dinosaur," said Brigid. "It's a real, living creature, and according to our telepath, it's full of rage and a desire to kill."

We all looked around for a minute until we realized that the "telepath" was Angel. Well, "telepath" sounds better than "creepy little mind-reading kid," so I was cool with it.

"But what do you think it is, Dr. Dwyer?" asked one of the other researchers.

"I think it's either a created life-form or a life-form that's been affected, mutated, or enhanced," she said, "by radiation."

"Created life-form?" One of the researchers frowned.

"Like us," I said. "Right? Ninety-eight percent human, two percent avian." Might as well name the elephant—or bird kid—in the room.

"Well, yes," Brigid said awkwardly, not looking at me. "Only not as successful. But I'm more inclined to think that it was an ordinary life-form that was irradiated and has mutated."

"Radiation?" Nudge asked. "Like, they microwaved it?"

"Not exactly," said Brigid. "There are many sources of radiation, both naturally occurring and man-made. I'm thinking of some of the mutations observed after Hiroshima and Chernobyl."

"I've heard those names before," I said, wondering if it had been on a TV show.

"Hiroshima is a town in Japan," John said. "The U.S. dropped a nuclear bomb on it near the end of World War II. The bomb killed a hundred thousand people outright, but tens of thousands more later from radiation sickness. Plus, as time went on, it became clear that lingering effects of radiation caused some human genes to mutate. This mostly showed up as birth defects, miscarriages, and cancerous tumors."

"Fun," I muttered.

"Chernobyl was a nuclear power plant in the Soviet Union," John went on. "The site of the worst nuclear-reactor accident in human history. The area around it is still contaminated with radiation, and it's unclear whether people will be able to live anywhere near it ever again. Huge amounts of radiation were released into the atmosphere and caused genetic problems and contaminated food and milk as far away as Sweden and England. The thing is, radiation can cause unpredictable and often fatal genetic mutations in living creatures."

"You're saying you think there's radiation in the ocean, and it caused these creatures to mutate into these attacking monsters?" a researcher asked.

Brigid nodded. "That's exactly what I'm saying. Now we just have to find out where the radiation is."

60

"I LIKE BOATS better than subs," I said.

I looked up at the sky above us, and back at the foamy white wake we were leaving behind us. I breathed in deeply, the fresh, salty air still seeming like heaven after being on the sub. We were on the marine research station's biggest boat, a forty-five-foot tri-hull that sliced neatly through the water.

"We're setting up the radiation-detecting equipment right now," said Brigid. "Fang, come see this—it's really interesting."

I bit my lip to keep from screaming. Fang shot me a sideways glance, then followed Brigid below deck to the equipment room.

Half an hour later we were far out into the ocean and

could barely see land, even with our raptor vision. The boat's engines stopped, but the water here was too deep for us to anchor. I couldn't help it—I ran down the deck of the boat, then leaped off the end, into the air.

Snapping out my wings, I rose on the ocean's thermal wind, climbing in lazy spirals toward the sun. In moments I was joined by Angel, Iggy, Gazzy, Nudge, and Total. Everyone but Fang. I tried not to think about him, his dark head bent toward Dr. Amazing's as they murmured about ocean maps. For now I just wanted to enjoy flying.

Six months ago, we'd flown just about every day, for hours. It had been our main mode of transport. My wings had felt strong, tireless. Some days it had actually felt weird to walk. Lately it seemed like I spent a lot of time in planes, on boats and subs, in cars. But today I could fly and enjoy the sun and exercise making heat radiate off my feathers.

"This feels good," said Iggy.

"Yeah," Gazzy agreed.

"I never want to wear khaki again," Nudge declared, swooping in a huge, freewheeling circle. For a while we'd lived among hawks and then with some bats. They'd taught us all kinds of maneuvers, and I always felt a burst of joy when I recognized them in the air.

These were the times when I didn't actually feel that human, and I could let go of some of my human problems. Like my mom being kidnapped. Or Fang and Brigid. Or my come-and-go Voice. Right now I could just—

"Agh!"

Something hard and wet exploded against my shoulder, drenching my shirt. I looked back frantically, hoping I wouldn't see a sprawling flow of blood. It seemed like . . . it seemed like . . .

I looked up to see Gazzy almost doubled in half, laughing so hard he was practically snorting. He got a grip on himself and whipped another water balloon out from under his jacket. Nudge squealed as he smacked her right in the head despite her evasive moves.

"My hair!" she shrieked, water dripping into her eyes. "You know what humidity does to it!"

Iggy cackled and pulled out his own arsenal. He and Gazzy pelted me, Nudge, and Angel over and over—I had no idea how they'd even reached that elevation carrying so much weight in water balloons. And where had they gotten the stupid balloons anyway? It wasn't like we'd popped into a party store lately!

"Ow!" I yelled. "Stop it, you two! I'm gonna get you!"

We played dive-bomb and chase, tag-a-feather, and had water-balloon wars for a good long while. At one point I'd grabbed Gazzy's leg, holding him upside down and shaking him to make his balloons fall. Nudge and Angel hovered below him, catching the ones that dropped, then humming them at Iggy and Gazzy.

Good, clean bird-kid fun was had by all. Except Fang.

Finally we swooped lower and lower, faces flushed, hair windblown, eyes bloodshot from the breeze, cheeks hurting from smiling so much and laughing so hard.

On the boat's deck, I saw Fang waiting, standing very still. Several researchers were holding binoculars, watching us fly back toward them. When we were about sixty feet away, Angel suddenly pointed.

"Look over there!" she called. "Something big and dark, not a whale!"

I looked and saw it: a huge, uneven shape, seeming to dive down deeper into the water. In another moment it was gone.

I landed gracefully on the boat's deck with barely a sound, like a little sparkly fairy or something. Let's see Dr. Stupendous do *that*.

"We just saw something in the water," I said, panting a little. "It went too deep for us to make it out, but there's definitely something there, not too far away."

"We need to go under and look for it," Angel said firmly, climbing up on the boat rail and preparing to jump.

"Hold it!" I said. "Let's come up with a plan before you jump in, okay?"

"I agree," said Brigid. "We're picking up radiation signals, but we can't tell where they're coming from. I'd like more time to explore that."

"Oh," said Angel, nodding, and I let out a breath at her apparent show of reasonableness, something that had been in short supply from her lately. "But *I'm* ready *now,*" she said, and hopped nimbly overboard, plunging quickly into the water.

I was gonna kill that kid.

61

I'D LIKE TO TAKE A MINUTE to point out that under water, humans need fins, a mask, a tank of compressed air, and a regulator to breathe from. Up in the air, I needed nothing. What does that tell you? *I was not meant to be under water.*

It took almost eight minutes for me, Fang, Dr. Akana, and John to get set up in scuba gear. It felt more like a month. But finally I was holding my mask against my face and falling backward over the side of the boat, feeling the weight belt and heavy scuba tank pulling me beneath the surface.

Three more splashes and then our gang of four did a 360, hoping against hope that Angel had lingered in the area.

How much do you wanna bet that she did, and that we spotted her right away, and that she agreed to stay with us nicely while we looked around under water?

Didn't think so. That mouthy six-, I mean *seven*-year-old—with a will of iron and all the calm reasoning power of your average rabid squirrel. Between that and her occasional bids to become the flock leader, she—was cruisin' for a bruisin'.

John and Dr. Akana pointed off into the distance and started to swim in that direction. Fang and I followed, because we sure didn't have any other options. Ahead of us were hills of coral or rock or something and a zillion fish swimming in and around and darting in and out of shallow cavelike places. Dr. Akana had told us that there were some volcanic caves in the waters around Hawaii, and I guessed that was what we were looking at.

But no Angel and not even a trail of bubbles to follow. We were all carrying powerful flashlights and now shone them into the caves, watching as fish startled over and over again. We saw lobsters, too many different kinds of fish to identify, corals, sponges, a couple of moray eels poking their heads out of their holes. But no Angel.

I was starting to get really mad, and this tank on my back made me feel awkward. The fact was, when it was just the six of us, Angel really listened to me and wanted to stay close by me. Now that we were surrounded by grown-ups who were giving us food and taking us on adventures, Angel didn't seem to need me as much. It hurt.

I flicked my light around a cave, saw nothing bird-kid-like, and started to back out. I glanced around for the others...and realized I was totally alone.

And way, way deep inside a cave.

I'd been caught up in my musings and had not seen the group moving off somewhere else. Backpedaling quickly, I looked right and left, searching the dark water for flashlight beams. I couldn't see anything. I couldn't even see the cave entrance. I must have wandered in there and gone around corners without realizing it.

Crap.

I deliberately slowed my breathing and tried to calm down. I got into this cave; I could get out. I had enough air in my tank for about half an hour, I thought. I've been in worse situations. I just needed to settle down and backtrack.

Of course, backtracking works best when there are footprints to follow, or when the terrain has landmarks and is therefore recognizable. It does not work when the only trail is bubbles, and every single rotten cave wall looks exactly like every *other* single rotten freaking cave wall, and there are only surprised fish to ask for directions and—oops!—*I'm not a freaking telepath!!!*

An underwater scream is *so* much less satisfying and effective when it is done into a regulator, I discovered.

Picturing Fang recovering my drowned body, I swam carefully back in the direction I thought I had come from. None of it looked familiar, and none of it *didn't* look familiar.

It all looked the same.

There was no light coming from anywhere, no sign of my fellow divers. I pictured my funeral, saw Nudge choking back sobs as she threw flowers on my coffin. My throat closed, and tears welled up in my eyes, which *made my mask fog up.*

I swore loudly into my regulator and cleared my mask the way I'd been taught. When I could see, I again tried to steady my breathing and take stock of where I was.

That's when I realized that I was looking ahead at two caves, where a branch veered off. Had I traveled down one of the branches, or had I come from somewhere behind me—should I turn around?

Let me rephrase that question: If my life were a corny horror movie, and the heroine was lost and alone, trapped in an underwater cave, what would happen next?

If you guessed, "She drops her flashlight, and it hits a rock and breaks, leaving her in utter darkness," you would be right.

But I bet you didn't guess the part about an attack by a giant octopus.

62

"JUST SIGN IT." The second-in-command pushed the paper across the table.

Dr. Valencia Martinez looked at the woman. Her hands were handcuffed behind her back again, and she was so tired. At least her actual hunger pangs had gone away after four days without food. Now she just felt weak and sick and like she wanted to sleep for a very long time. "No."

The second-in-command sat back. "All you have to do is sign and then appear on camera denouncing your work at the Coalition to Stop the Madness. Then you can eat and drink, and we will return you to your family."

Just the idea of eating actual food made Dr. Martinez feel sick. "No. I believe in the CSM. We're destroying our planet, and it has to stop."

The second-in-command was careful not to show her frustration and anger. Instead, she nodded at one of the M-Geeks standing guard. It moved forward smoothly, its wheels making no sound. It reached out an arm, and a long, thin screwdriver-like thing extended from the end. It touched the skin on Dr. Martinez's arm and emitted a shock.

She jumped but stifled a shriek of pain. The tool left a small red mark on her arm, next to all the other small red marks. *I look like I have the measles,* she thought with rising hysteria. *Think about something else,* she told herself. *Be somewhere else.*

The small, stuffy room seemed to fade away as Valencia looked past the second-in-command, out through the small, thick window. The water outside was dark: the only light came from the powerful beams of this underwater station. Dr. Martinez wished they would just shoot her out into the water, the way they had the fourth-in-command. It would be heavenly out there, quiet and cold and wet, and as soon as she was out there, it would be over. She wouldn't have to worry anymore. They couldn't hurt her anymore. She could sleep.

Something enormous and dark moved through one of the beams of light. Valencia blinked, seeing that it wasn't a whale. What on earth was it? It was alive, not a machine, but like nothing Valencia had ever seen or heard of. It was . . . an abomination, a grotesque mistake.

And suddenly, everything clicked into place, everything

made sense, and she knew why they had kidnapped her, why they were holding her, and why they desperately needed the CSM to stop its protesting.

"If you don't want to save yourself," said the second-in-command, "you might want to save your eldest daughter."

Dr. Martinez met her captor's eyes. "What?"

"We have Maximum Ride in custody," said the second-in-command triumphantly. "Sign this, and we will let her go."

Laughter croaked out of Dr. Martinez's dry mouth, distracting her from her pain and weakness. "If you've got Max in custody," she said, "then you have my sympathy."

She started to laugh again, but the M-Geek shocked her much more strongly now, and everything went fuzzy for a minute, before she passed out.

63

OKAY, I'm no marine biologist, so the whole octopus/squid distinction is lost on me. All I can tell you is that it was way bigger than me, gushy, slippery, impossible to get hold of, and seemed to have a million tentacley arms that it wrapped so tightly around me I couldn't move.

I remembered how octopi and squid eat their prey—they pry open clams and use their sucky arms to shove the soft clam meat into their parrotlike beaks. It was trying to pry me open! Then it would stuff soft bird-kid meat into its beak!

I drew in panicked breaths from the regulator, thrashing around, trying to kick backward, everything I could think of to break free.

Reminder: One cannot build up a lot of power in water.

One cannot jump up and kick something. One cannot use one's weight effectively. One can only thrash around, pushing helplessly against gushy, squishy, stretchy tentacles, trying to pry them off of everything.

One can also try to reach the eight-inch knife one has strapped to one's thigh. Of course, I couldn't get mine, because that was how *this whole day* had gone.

And then it pulled my mask right off my face.

Cold salty water splashed into my eyes, went up my nose. Meanwhile, the slimy beast pulled the regulator out of my mouth, almost yanking my teeth along with it as I tried to hold on. Now I had no air source.

I pressed my lips together so I wouldn't swallow the salt water. We mutant freaks have very efficient lungs and air sacs, but we do have to breathe. If I couldn't breathe, I would drown, here in a dark cave, lost and alone.

Without ever kissing Fang again.

Tears are kind of redundant in the ocean, but I felt them well up hotly in my eyes.

64

EYES SQUEEZED shut, mouth closed tightly, I struggled with all my might, wishing with every fiber of my being that this was a plain-old regular Eraser or Flyboy or M-Geek or clone or any other ridiculous, stupid thing that someone had thought up—

The arms loosened their hold on me.

I fought and struggled again, and the arms loosened some more. Then suddenly the arms were gone. I lunged for my regulator hose and saw that the cave was full of light.

And there were John, Dr. Akana, and Fang. I had opened my eyes just in time to see Fang punching the octopus/squid/cephalopod right in its big googly eyes.

I reached around and grabbed my regulator—only to

find half of a ripped hose, which had blown my entire air supply out in a huge, festive burst of bubbles.

A couple more punches and the thing turned and fled into the darkness. Fang swam over to me quickly, seeing my air hose, my breath-holding face probably turning purple. John and Dr. Akana came over too, indicating which way led out of the cave.

Then Fang's eyes crinkled behind his mask: he was smiling.

Smiling? I had, like, five seconds to go before my lungs exploded. Were my last thoughts as a living bird kid going to be, *I thought you loved me, Fang, you freaking traitor?!*

Then he took my hand in his and gently ran his fingers along the sides of my neck.

My eyes widened. I could just barely feel a steady stream of tiny bubbles brushing past my fingers. I did a systems check: Did I feel like I was about to pass out from lack of oxygen? Did my lungs feel like they were about to burst?

Nah, not really.

I grinned back at Fang.

I had developed gills.

65

I REMEMBERED how Angel had demonstrated this new talent—she sort of gulped in big mouthfuls of water, and they seemed to flow out her almost-invisible gills. I tried that, tentatively, fearing if I swallowed a bunch of salt water I would immediately gag.

But there was some new mechanism in place, and though I gulped in water, it immediately shot back out again, not down my windpipe or my esophagus.

It was so, so cool. Grinning, I unfastened my vest and let it and my tank drop below me into the depths. I felt so much better, lighter, and more maneuverable without it.

Then I leaned closer to Fang, peering through the water at his neck, smooth and tan under my pruney fingers. I pulled back and smiled at him, nodding. He had the same stream of bubbles seeping out from the sides of his neck.

He spit out his regulator, as John and Dr. Akana swam toward him in alarm. They tried to stop him from ditching his tank, but he pointed to his neck, and began to take water into his mouth. The scientists' eyes grew huge behind their masks.

Looking stunned, they motioned toward the mouth of the cave. And who was waiting for us there, blond curls floating dreamily in the water like an impish mermaid?

Yeah. Angel. And when she saw us without our air tanks, she grinned in an incredibly annoying, see-I-told-you-so way. Little twerp.

As we moved toward her, I started to get the whole gill pattern of breathing down—take in a big mouthful of water, sort of swallow it, feel it flow out through the gills on the sides of my neck.

In another minute, it had become smoother and more instinctual, and I rejoiced in how incredibly cool and handy this new skill would be...and then, of course, immediately began to fear that I'd start sprouting other fish traits. Like scales.

Uh, like, no thank you.

But swimming with no bulky, heavy tank, no rubber mouthpiece making my jaw ache—I started to see what Angel found so amazing about being under water. I still totally preferred the air environment, with my wings stretched out in the sun. But this wasn't so bad.

The five of us backtracked, heading to the boat. I started to compose a lengthy lecture for Angel, during which I planned to sit her down and try to drum some sense into her scary little head.

And then, with no warning, something broadsided me so hard it knocked the breath out of wherever I was holding it these days.

66

THE PROJECTILE WAS AS BIG and fast as a freight train and just as powerful. Ramming my side, it tore me far away from the others, making me turn somersaults and startling me so much that I gulped in water and actually swallowed it.

Without my bulky air tank, I quickly managed to right myself and assumed a fighting stance. I was maybe twenty feet away from everyone else, and they were under attack too.

But what was attacking us? The thing that had hit me had turned back toward the others with startling speed. I immediately shot after it, keeping my wings tight against my back, reminding myself to breathe.

The creatures were bizarrely agile and fast, whipping

through the water like snakes or eels. And they came in sizes, ranging from Volkswagen bug to Boeing 747. I suspected they were what had attacked the fishing boats and the navy sub, but even this close, I couldn't identify what they were.

I jumped onto one's back, trying to hold on as I pummeled it as hard as I could. Its skin was bumpy and rough—and this close much of it looked melted and raw, with enormous, festering wounds that turned my stomach. I tried to find eyes to punch or poke, tried to see some vulnerable underside, but it was just—all muddled up. There was no pattern or symmetry.

The thing bucked and threw me off, and I swirled fast and shot over to where Fang was entangled with one that had flippers. I leaned back and kicked it as hard as I could, and this time I saw a small red eye on one side. Just the one eye.

A quick glance revealed that John and Dr. Akana were already panicked and nearing exhaustion, thrashing around in the water, unsuccessfully trying to fend off blows. We'd been steadily climbing to the surface and now could see pretty clearly, but there was no sign of the boat above us. I had no idea where the heck we were or how I could summon help.

Even Angel seemed to be under attack, and I wondered if these creatures were completely beyond any kind of communication.

Max. Get out of there now! the Voice suddenly commanded. *Get the others, and get out of there now!*

I grabbed Angel's shoulder and shoved her up toward the surface, meanwhile kicking the sea monster that surged after her.

I gave a two-handed karate chop across the snout of another creature, freeing John, then pushed him up until he caught on. Fang had finally kicked himself free of his beast, though it was circling to come after him again. Together he and I punched and chopped and kicked the one that had almost knocked Dr. Akana unconscious.

I heard a thin, sharp whistling sound and looked around to see a slim, dark, long thing coming right at us. Not an animal but even more deadly: a torpedo. The navy had arrived.

"Up!" I yelled at Fang, bubbles leaving my mouth. "Now!!"

We spun away from the sea monsters, grabbed Dr. Akana, and kicked as hard as we could toward the surface. Some of them started to come after us, and Fang grabbed my other hand, using his strength to pull me up with him. We put about thirty feet between us and the creatures, feeling our ears pop painfully as the water pressure lessened.

We almost managed to get out of range but not quite. Below us, the torpedo hit the pod of creatures, creating a tremendous explosion that blasted me and Fang right out of the water and about twenty feet into the air. I cried out, holding my ears, then realized I was airborne. I quickly extended my wings and shook the water off.

Fang did the same, and we kept ourselves aloft high

above the ocean, watching as big chunks of monster bobbed to the surface. The sub that had launched the torpedo was too far away to see.

I could barely hear anything and felt like someone had hammered an ice pick through my eardrums. It hurt so much that tears came to my eyes—even swallowing hurt.

Less than a quarter mile away, the boat was cranking its engines. Fang and I flew over to it and landed on the deck. We were both covered with scrapes and bruises, I'd swallowed a bunch of water, and my head was spinning from the pain in my ears. All in all, I felt like crap, though maybe not as bad as Dr. Akana, who had been fished out of the water and was now strapped to a body board.

Panting, I leaned against the side of the boat and looked at Fang.

"So the navy stepped up after all," I said, my voice sounding muffled and far away to me. "Humans actually saved us. In a messy, stupid way, but still."

This was a new concept, and it took us a moment to digest it. But we had a much more important question: what the heck were those things, and *where had they come from?*

67

"WELCOME BACK," said Captain Perry. He was—I swear—trying not to smirk at me.

I snarled as I went past him, took a deep breath, and started down the submarine's ladder.

Yes. Back on a submarine. A much smaller sub but again one of the navy's and again commanded by Captain Joshua Perry.

Turned out only one of my eardrums was busted. It would heal pretty quickly, but in the meantime I was staggering around like a deaf, drunk monkey.

Dr. Akana had a broken arm and collarbone, and bruises covered almost half her body. She'd been airlifted back to the marine research station. John Abate was also beat up and bruised but was still with us, determined to see this thing through to the end, determined to save my mom. I was starting to wonder if maybe he had feelings for her, I mean, more than just a friend and co-worker.

There was a lot of that going around.

We'd spent the night at the marine research station, going over everything we had learned so far, which could be summed up in like two sentences: (1) these things were ginormously gol dang big, and (2) we had no idea what the heck they were.

I'd managed to get most of my lecture in with Angel, but my words slid right off her like rain off a road slick. I was going to ask Fang to try talking to her.

Gazzy, Iggy, and Nudge had all tried to see if they had gills, out in the warm, clear water of the bay. That's another body of water you'll never catch me swimming in again. Turns out none of them were turning fishy yet.

Total had elected to stay at the research station with Akila. He hated subs—no one's blaming him there—and hated water and had no gills and needed some catch-up time with his lady friend, as he put it. He was still wrestling with the whole marriage question.

The submarine crew was no doubt used to top-secret missions where they just did as ordered without asking questions—another thing the military seemed big on—but, all the same, when they saw that their new passengers were six kids and two scientists, their eyes got a little bigger.

Now, hours later, we all huddled over a lit map-table in

a small room in the midsection of the sub. This sub was so small that it held only about thirty people and actually had a few thick windows. It was still armed with torpedoes, though, which made me feel better.

"The monster attacks occurred here, here, and here," said Captain Perry, showing us red dots on the maps. "All within a twenty-mile radius. Today we're going to cruise this area, crisscrossing it until we see something."

"I still think these creatures were caused by radiation poisoning," said Brigid. "We definitely get high radiation levels around here, but it's been mysteriously difficult to pinpoint."

"Could I go outside and just hang on to one of the sub's fins?" Angel asked. "Then I could really see stuff."

"No," Captain Perry, John, and I all said at the same time.

Angel frowned.

"The ones I saw up close had wounds all over their skin," I said. "They were like building-sized pickles, except their pickley skin was all messed up, raw and bleeding and oozing. It was horrible."

"Did you pick up on anything from them, Angel?" Brigid asked. "The first time, you felt their rage and their desire to kill. Did you get anything different yesterday?"

"Uh-huh," said Angel. "They were still mad and wanted to kill us, but they're also in pain. And they're smart. They can communicate with each other and make plans, work together to attack us in a group. They're kind of neat—more understandable than whales or dolphins."

"Uh, what?" John said.

"Whales are great and all, but everything about them is *really* slow," Angel said matter-of-factly. "They take forever to get a thought across. And dolphins—well, they're kind of flighty. They just want to have fun. It's hard to get them to focus on anything. Unless you're constantly flinging fish at them. They're big into rewards."

"I see," said John.

Just then a machine started pinging quickly. Brigid rushed to it.

"Off-the-scale radiation, right here," she said excitedly. "Turn on the floodlights, and let's see what's going on."

Captain Perry quickly gave the command, and the undersea world around us was illuminated with powerful lights. We all raced to the few small windows and peered out as the brightness swept back and forth like a beacon.

"And there it is," said John, sounding depressed. "One mystery solved."

68

"WHAT ARE WE looking at?" Gazzy asked.

"I'm guessing... fish?" Iggy said, sounding bored.

"There's a bunch of containers out on the ocean floor," I explained to him. "Plus fish."

"How deep are we?" Nudge asked, her nose pressed against the thick glass.

"Almost a thousand meters," said Captain Perry. "More than three thousand feet. Not the deepest part of the ocean by any means but still deeper than most subs can go."

"So they were counting on people not being likely to find it," Fang said.

"Yes," Brigid murmured, staring out the window.

"We're moving in closer," said Captain Perry.

"There's writing on the containers," I said.

"Shining lights on it now," said Captain Perry.

This close, with the floodlights hitting them full on, we could see dim markings on the sides and tops of the barrels. Brigid's radiation detector was practically in hysterics, and I wanted to say, "Okay! We get it! There's radiation! Now shut up!"

"There are Chinese characters," said John.

I looked at the barrels and saw they were also stenciled with English words. "It says, Danger, Keep Away." I read slowly, peering through the water. "Property of the Chu Corporation. Huh. No surprise there. And they're marked with some kind of yellow and black sign."

"That's the symbol for radioactive material," said Brigid.

"Some of the containers' lids are popped," said Gazzy. "Like they've rusted open. I assume that's an 'uh-oh' kind of thing."

"I guess you were right about the radiation causing the monsters," said Nudge.

"It hasn't been proved yet," said Brigid. "A scientist needs conclusive proof. But it does certainly look possible."

"It's all making sense now," said John. "The Chu Corporation is dumping illegal radioactive material into the ocean. He created his army of robots to keep it hidden and protected. The CSM was doing a lot of work to bring ocean pollution to everyone's notice, so we became a threat." He rubbed his hands over his eyes, looking tired.

"Now what?" said Iggy. "Who you gonna call?"

A quiet voice in the hallway outside said, "Ghost-busters!"

Captain Perry and John groaned. "That phrase is ruined forever," said John.

"Well, let's get back up to the surface," I said briskly, trying not to sound too eager. Knowing I could breathe under water was comforting, but at this depth, if I went out of the sub, I'd be mushed flatter than a pancake in less than a second. "We can call the EPA or the CSM or the navy or whoever, and tell them where this stuff is."

Not so easy, Max, said the Voice. *It's never that easy. You should know that.*

Okay, who saw that coming? Be honest. Everyone but me?

"Uh-oh," said Angel.

"Double uh-oh," said Gazzy.

I rushed back to the window and looked out, cupping my hands around my eyes. The sea was moving. Wait—no, not the sea...

It was a wave of Mr. Chu's weatherproof all-terrain assassins. There were hundreds of them, and they were rushing toward the sub.

It was battle time. Again.

69

CAPTAIN PERRY HIT the intercom. "Prepare for attack! This is not a drill! Repeat, this is not a drill! We are at DEFCON one! Arm the torpedoes, and plot evasive action!"

There was a scurry of activity as men rushed to their battle stations.

The first M-Geeks hit the sides of the sub, and we all grabbed on to something. I happened to grab on to Fang. We couldn't just go out into the water and fight them, not at this depth, with its crushing pressure. So if I was about to die a horrible watery death *again,* this time I didn't want to go out alone. I wanted to be with Fang and the rest of the flock.

Alarms were sounding, people were shouting, and we heard the first clanging, grinding noises of the M-Geeks trying to breach the sub's hull. (That's fancy sailor talk for them trying to punch a hole in the boat's side, so we would all drown.) This seems to be a glaringly obvious weakness of the whole submarine concept. I'm just saying.

"You kids stay here!" commanded Captain Perry, starting to head up to the control room.

"Um—if I might make a suggestion," said Gazzy.

"No time, kid," said the captain, half out the door.

"You should listen to this," said Iggy firmly, and there was something determined about his face and sightless blue eyes that made the captain pause.

"What?" he asked tensely.

"This one time, when we were surrounded by M-Geeks, there was a storm coming, and we rigged a delayed-timer electricity booster," Gazzy explained. "When lightning hit the rod, it was amplified, and we aimed it at the M-Geeks. They all, like, turned inside out, and fried. It was excellent." He beamed at the memory, and he and Iggy slapped high fives.

"That was good thinking, son," said the captain, "but I don't see how that helps us now."

"You've got *torpedoes*," said Iggy, as if this made it all perfectly clear.

"Torpedoes are good at hitting a particular target," said the captain. "These things are many smaller targets, and they're in direct contact with our ship. We can't do anything to them without harming ourselves."

I groaned to myself as I recognized the exaggerated patience of a grown-up who can't comprehend the fact that eight-year-old Gazzy and fourteen-year-old Iggy probably knew more about demolitions, detonators, and explosive devices than almost anyone else on earth.

"No, no," said Iggy. "You take the detonator out, then wire it directly to the sub's hull."

"If you want to give it extra oomph, take the actual explosive stuff, like the ammonium nitrate stuff, and diffuse it throughout the water," suggested Gazzy. "Then, when you electrify the metal hull, it'll ignite and spread the damage out into the water, but not too far, and you'll take out mostly M-Geeks, since I bet they probably scared off most fish in the area."

Captain Perry just looked at Gazzy, and then at Iggy, and blinked a couple times.

"They're really good at this," I said, as the grinding and clanging got louder. "They like to . . . blow up things."

"We know how to do it lots of different ways," Gazzy said eagerly.

Captain Perry paused for a moment, then got on the intercom. "Lieutenant Youngville, report to the map room!" He turned back to us. "She's our demolitions master."

A moment later, a harried-looking young woman with short brown hair came in and saluted.

"At ease," said Captain Perry. "Young man, explain your theory to Lieutenant Youngville. Fast."

Gazzy did.

It took the lieutenant a minute to digest what Gazzy and Iggy said. Then she nodded slowly. "You're a diabolical little pyro, aren't you?" she asked Gazzy.

He blushed modestly.

"Let's do this thing!" the lieutenant yelled, running out of the room.

It was barely three minutes later when a huge *flash!* from outside lit our small room like lightning. It had seemed much longer — listening to the grinding, scraping sounds, wondering how quickly the M-Geeks would punch through. Then tiny, crackling lights skittered through the water. We waited anxiously.

Seconds later, there was a larger series of popping explosions as the torpedo's powdered explosive drifted out into the water, where it was detonated by the electrical sparks still dancing around the metal hull of the sub. Gazzy crowed and held up his hand to slap high fives with the captain, who just looked at him.

"It's like M-Geek popcorn," Iggy said, as we heard a fast string of small booms, one after another, each accompanied by a flash of light.

"Yeah," Gazzy chimed in excitedly. "It's like an *ignart!*"

I was about to say that this was no time for fart jokes when the grinding metal sounds stopped abruptly.

"It seems to be working, sir," reported Lieutenant Youngville, poking her head into the map room. "The technique—"

"The Gaz-Ig-Nart technique!" Iggy corrected.

"Yes, the Gaz-Ig-Nart technique seems to be neutralizing the enemy," the lieutenant finished.

The captain tried. We all tried. But there was no way. When the ensign came to report, he found us all laughing so hard we had tears coming out of our eyes.

70

"WE'RE GOING TO RETURN to base now to make a formal report," Captain Perry said once he'd gotten his voice back.

"Wait—what about finding my mom?" I asked.

"She's got to be around here somewhere," John agreed. "Can you wait on that report so we can comb the area more thoroughly?"

"There's leaking radioactive waste out there," said Captain Perry. "Who knows where that radiation is ending up, how far it can travel? It must be contained as soon as possible."

"We came out here to find our colleague," John said.

"My job is to protect the United States, which Hawaii and its surrounding waters are part of," said Captain Perry, looking steely eyed.

I was calculating the chances of success if the bird kids staged a mutiny and seized control of the submarine, when Nudge suddenly said, “Where’s Angel?”

And if those words don’t strike terror into your heart by now, then you haven’t been paying attention.

It took barely two minutes to search the entire sub. The systems engineer determined that someone had opened the diver’s air lock approximately four minutes before.

“She couldn’t have gone out into the ocean!” the captain said, horrified. “The pressure at this depth is tons per square inch. She’d be crushed instantly!!”

“Or... not,” I said, looking out the window. The water, even with the floodlights shining into it, was cloudy and hard to see through. It was still full of bits o’ ’bots, drifting downward like evil, metallic rain. Plus, all the explosions had stirred up aeons of debris on the ocean floor.

Even so, I could see the light color of the small jumpsuit Angel had been wearing, and the flash of gold as her hair floated around her like a halo that she *so* did not deserve. She was dog-paddling away from the sub, looking extremely uncrushed and three-dimensional.

“That’s... impossible,” Captain Perry said, sounding stunned.

“Totally and completely impossible,” John agreed, staring out the window in awe. “There’s no way anyone could be out at this depth without a pressure suit and survive. It—it just can’t be done.”

“Hello?” I said. “We’re children with *wings*. And now

gills. We *fly*. Angel can read minds and communicate with fish, Iggy can feel colors, Nudge can draw metal to her, and now you're saying that there's simply no way Angel could be out there? Have I mentioned the *wings* part?"

John nodded, still looking shocked. "But still—this defies any kind of understanding we have of vertebrate animals. It's...almost impossible to comprehend."

"You mean, more than the freaking *wings?*"

Captain Perry looked at me seriously. "Yes, actually. More than the wings. This is, in fact, stranger and more impossible."

"Oh," I said. "Well, then." I gave a little cough. "Anyway, let's get her back in. You got any of those claw-arm thingies?"

"No, I'm afraid not," said Captain Perry.

"Max," said Nudge. She turned away from the window with wide eyes. I hurried over and peered out into the murky water.

"Oh, jeez," I said, my heart sinking. Or rather, sinking more.

Angel, being Angel, was being: (1) stubborn, (2) a rule breaker, (3) not sensible, (4) reckless,...and (5)...swimming directly at a group of the sea monsters, who were heading toward our sub at light speed.

"They're gonna kill her," Gazzy breathed, his face pale.

Yeah, I thought grimly. *And then I'll bring her back to life and kill her again, for doing this to us.*

One of the creatures spotted Angel. It slowed, turned, and began to head toward her.

"Oh, God," Nudge squealed, covering her eyes. "Max! Do something!"

I was already striding toward the door. "On it."

71

I SLAMMED MY FIST against the pressure pad that opened the air-lock chamber. I knew Captain Perry and the others were right behind me, and if they wanted to get sucked out of the diver air lock along with me, that was their business.

Ten seconds ago, one of those creatures had been speeding toward Angel. That image, seared into my brain, made me feel sick. I couldn't believe that after all we'd been through, everything we'd done, Angel had basically just committed suicide by sea monster.

The air-lock door opened, the interior of the chamber still wet from Angel's escape.

Brigid grabbed my arm. "Max—don't," she said. "You know you can't go up against them. The best thing would be for us to get out of here, fast, before they start attacking the whole sub. Remember what they did to the *Minnesota?* This one is so much smaller and more vulnerable."

"I have to go get Angel," I snarled with my endearing bulldog tenacity.

"Max—you can't help her." Brigid sounded close to tears.

"I'm not leaving her," I said, standing threateningly over Brigid, several inches taller. "If it's too late, then I'm bringing back her body. Either way, I'm not leaving without her." I looked at Captain Perry, John, Brigid, and the rest of the flock. "So suck it up and get out of my way."

John looked at me for a long moment, then nodded, and carefully stepped out of the air-lock chamber. He touched Captain Perry's arm, and, frowning, Captain Perry left too.

"Brigid," said John. Tears rolling down her cheeks, she let go of my arm and left the room, followed by a solemn, stiff-jawed flock.

Except Fang.

I glared at him. "Go on. Try to stop me. I dare you." It was like the old days when we used to wrestle, each trying to get the better of the other. I was ready to take him down, my hands curled into fists.

"I was just going to say be careful," Fang told me. He stepped closer and brushed some hair out of my eyes. "And—I've got your back." He motioned with his head toward the torpedo chamber.

Oh, my God. It hit me like a tsunami then: how perfect he was for me, how no one else would ever, could ever be so perfect for me, how he was everything I could possibly hope for, as a friend, boyfriend—maybe even more. He was it for me. There would be no more looking.

I really, really loved him, with a whole new kind of love I'd never felt before, something that made every other kind of love I'd ever felt just seem washed out and wimpy in comparison. I loved him with every cell in my body, every thought in my head, every feather in my wings, every breath in my lungs. And air sacs.

Too bad I was going out to face almost certain death.

Right there, in front of everyone, I threw my arms around his neck and smashed my mouth against his. He was startled for a second, then his strong arms wrapped around me so tightly I could hardly breathe.

"ZOMG," I heard Nudge whisper, but still Fang and I kissed, slanting our heads this way and that to get closer. I could have stood there and kissed him happily for the next millennium, but Angel—or what was left of her—was still out there in the cold, dark ocean.

Reluctantly, I ended the kiss, took a step back. Fang's obsidian eyes were glittering brightly, and his stoic face had a look of wonder on it.

"Gotta go," I said quietly.

A half smile quirked his mouth. "Yeah. Hurry back."

I nodded, and he stepped out of the air-lock chamber, keeping his eyes fixed on me, memorizing me, as he hit the switch that sealed the chamber. The doors hissed shut with a kind of finality, and I realized my heart was beating so hard it felt like it was going to start snapping ribs.

I was scared.

I was crazily, deeply, incredibly, joyously, terrifiedly in love.

I was on a death mission.

Before my head simply exploded from too much emotion, I hit the large button that pressurized the air lock enough for the doors to open to the ocean outside. I really, really hoped that I would prove to be somewhat uncrushable, like Angel did.

The doors cracked open below me, and I saw the first dark glint of frigid water.

Showtime, folks.

72

THE ARTIFICIAL AIR PRESSURE in the chamber allowed me to drop down into the water. Want to hear something funny? I took a deep breath first. Then I remembered I didn't have to.

Then every thought went right out of my mind as I realized how totally completely *beyond* cold the water was at this depth. I gurgled out my best underwater shriek, realized I hadn't been crushed yet, and began to swim toward the light.

I was hoping it was the sub's floodlights and not the lights of the afterlife, like I'd already just died and didn't realize it and now I was swimming toward, well, I guess not heaven, even on a good day, but someplace lighter than the other option at least. Then I realized that if I was already dead, I wouldn't feel like a bird-kid-cicle, so cold that every tiny movement was incredibly painful. So that cheered me up.

At this depth, even though I hadn't been crushed, it was still shockingly hard to swim, to move, to get anywhere. It was like paddling through Jell-O or in slow motion, and there *was* a lot of weight pressing in on me on all sides. It didn't feel good, and I wondered how long my body would hold out.

The water was cloudy, full of debris, and I blinked constantly, wishing I'd remembered to put on a mask before I went charging off on my white seahorse. Then I saw it: one of the creatures. There were several more, grouped around it, but it was the biggest one, easily as big as our sub. It fixed its red eye on me, turning slightly.

The birds are working, said the Voice.

Huh? I was so startled that I quit swimming for a second.

The birds are working, the Voice repeated.

I began swimming again. *Voice, could we do this later? I'm kind of in the middle of something here.*

I was now about twenty feet away from the sea creature, and as before, I saw its skin was a mass of oozing sores, red-rimmed and raw. It wasn't symmetrical with a fin on each side—it looked like it had been put together by a two-year-old using a sea-monster Playmobil set. And he'd put it together wrong.

The birds are working, the Voice repeated. *They're working to help us.*

Just then the creature shifted, releasing . . . Angel.

I surged forward as fast as I could, which was about the pace of a sea slug. Angel's eyes were closed, and she floated there without moving. My heart constricted, and I paddled harder.

Then she blinked, smiled up at the sea monster, and turned to see me. Her face lit up, and she held out her arms, kicking off from the thing and rushing in slow motion toward me. I grabbed her and held her in a fierce hug, so relieved that she was still alive and that I could kick her butt later.

"Max!" she said, her small arms looped around my neck. It was bubbly and indistinct but understandable. "I've been explaining everything to Gor, here." She gestured at the biggest creature.

"Wha?" I managed.

"It isn't their fault," bubbled Angel. "They're genetic freaks, just like us. And they're smart. They've been attacking fishing boats because the long nets have been damaging their eggs and babies."

My mouth had dropped open, and now I quickly shut it as some tiny transparent shrimp tried to swim in.

"All the radiation created them, but it's also making them sick," Angel explained as minuscule bubbles wafted away from her neck. "They're really mad at the Chu Corporation. I told them we are too. So now we're on the same team! Plus—" Angel paused, her blue eyes gleaming in the floodlights. "Plus, they know where Dr. Martinez is."

73

"GOR SAYS IT'S NOT much farther," said Angel. She was wrapped in a towel, hair still wet, sipping a mug of hot tea. I was next to her, doing all the same things, except I wasn't communicating telepathically with a radiation-created, man-killing monster. I guess I do have limitations.

We were moving slowly through the darkness, our lights turned off as we tried to sneak up on Mr. Chu's under-water lair in a six-hundred-ton sub.

Angel's eyes unfocused, and she said, "It should be up here, on the left. Go really slow."

The captain gave the command, then handed out night-vision goggles, which Gazzy had been begging for for years. If the captain was smart, he'd count them all before we got off the sub.

"There it is," said Angel. "Gor and the others are going to wait here."

In the distance, we saw something that looked like it was out of a James Bond movie: an enormous clear-topped dome, three thousand feet below the sea. It looked like someone had covered over a football stadium and dropped it into the ocean. It was designed to blend in with its surroundings, and without the night goggles, we could have swum within fifty feet of it and not necessarily seen it.

As we got closer I could tell that the whole dome wasn't clear—it was metal on top, with a wide band of windows around the middle. Three different air-lock entries would admit submarines, which meant Mr. Chu had access to extradeep-diving subs. Maybe he had connections with some military organization? Maybe he was so stinking rich that he had bought his own private fleet of submarines?

"I can barely hear Gor," Angel said in frustration. She stood up and dropped her towel. "I have to go out again."

I had forty-thousand tons of reasons why I didn't want her to go back out, but we were actually relying on the recon abilities of the sea monsters (who called themselves the Krelp, by the way).

Instead I accepted the inevitable, including the even more gross inevitability that I should go out with her.

"Yeah, okay," I said, reluctantly unwrapping my towel. "I'll go with you."

"Oh, thanks, Max!" Angel took my hand and skipped alongside me as we headed for the air-lock chamber. It was like old times, except we were at the bottom of the ocean, talking to sea monsters, and about to rescue my kidnapped mother. Other than that, it was all old hat.

No one protested or tried to stop us this time. Fang looked at me, hope in his eyes, and I smirked at him. I save the huge emotional kissy-face for imminent death scenes. This probably didn't qualify.

I hoped. I really, really hoped.

74

SADLY, THE TEMPERATURE of the ocean water had not mysteriously risen by, say, fifty degrees while we were back on the sub. It was still horribly, teeth-chatteringly cold, and I went ahead and indulged myself in a searing tirade about cold water as we slowly swam toward the huge dome.

A hundred yards in back of us, the sub was still dark, blending in with the black water. I knew they were watching us with night-vision goggles, so I tried to look more heroic and less weeniefied about the cold.

The dome was lit and divided into rooms. Whatever glass-type stuff they had used was a couple of feet thick, and the interior was dim and distorted. Cautiously, Angel and I began to swim around the whole dome, seeing a room full of computers and equipment, another room full of sleeping dumb-bots, some rooms that looked like an apartment.

Finally, when we had swum almost the whole way around, I grabbed Angel's arm and pointed. There were several small, grayish compartments, set off from the others. In one of them, a slight figure lay curled on its side on the floor. It had long, dark, curly hair. *It was my mom*. Was she still alive?

Angel's eyes were big as we hovered there.

The glass is way too thick to break, I thought, and Angel nodded.

If we use a torpedo, it would probably kill my mom. Angel nodded again.

Maybe I could borrow some kind of big drill from the sub? Maybe we could storm in through an air lock? Angel frowned, unsure.

Then I noticed something weird. Okay, I mean, something *weirder*. There were no fish anywhere close to the dome. No nothing. This deep, it isn't exactly teeming with the circle of sea life anyway, but there were still plenty of freakish, scary things swimming around, not necessarily related to the oozing radiation. But none would come close to the dome, and no barnacles, sea stars, or tube worms attached themselves to it either.

Almost as soon as I realized that, the mystery was solved for us: an eel-like thing swam close and passed us. Then, *zap!* Some sort of invisible force field suddenly electrified it, killing it instantly. It sparked, twitched, then sank silently down into the depths to the ocean bottom.

Angel and I backed up several yards.

So much for attacking through the sub's air locks, I thought. My mom was right there! But I couldn't get to her. She was lying there so limp, unmoving—surely she was still alive. They couldn't have killed her yet, could they?

Angel looked perplexed, then turned her head and peered out into the darkness. Way off, using raptor vision, I could just barely make out the looming dark pickle shapes of the Krelp. Angel stared at them, cocking her head, as if she were listening. After a minute, she nodded.

The Krelp say they want to help, she thought at me.

But how? I asked.

I don't know, she answered.

I felt a swell of icy water push against me, and then the largest Krelp, the one Angel called Gor, surged past us, almost tumbling us head over heels. It neared the dome, got zapped over and over again, but steamrollered right through the force field.

Follow it! Angel commanded. *It's shorted out the electric net!*

We rushed after it, trying to trace its exact path. I braced myself for a horrible electrocution, but nothing happened. I swam as fast as I could to the window leading into my mom's cell. I rapped on it hard, but she didn't move.

Gor pressed itself against the glass, and I could only

imagine what it looked like from the inside. Someone inside the dome noticed it and started screaming. I saw people starting to race around, saw someone outside the room that housed all the sleeping 'bots. Still, my mom lay motionless.

My stomach got a cold, clenched feeling. Maybe, after all this, we were too late.

People were still staring up at the enormous creature pressed against the glass, and now I noticed a thick slime seeping out from under its body. This thing was the size of a 747. I mean, the word *eew* doesn't even come close.

"Watch," Angel said out loud.

Where the slime was touching the glass, wisps of smoke were twisting away into the water.

"Oh, my God," I said. "It's melting the glass with its... uh, body snot."

"Gazzy will be so jealous," Angel bubbled. "He'd give anything to be able to do that."

"Please do not tell him about it."

The glass continued to melt, and then something clicked in my brain, and I realized what would happen once the glass failed: water would seep in, then it would flood in, then it would crush the dome, and everything inside with its unimaginable weight.

If my mom wasn't dead now, she would be, really soon.

75

"ANGEL!" I yelled. Her head whipped around, floating gold curls wreathing her face. "We need the sub here, now! With its air lock open!"

Looking scared, Angel nodded. Her eyes unfocused as she compelled the crew back on the sub to come get us. I could almost feel its superquiet engines as they powered up.

Angel pressed her fingers to her temples as if she had a headache. Just as the first small trickle of ocean water began to seep into the dome, I was suddenly surrounded by Krelp.

Inside the dome, people were running and screaming. They didn't exactly have the navy's precise protocols of emergency preparedness. I looked for Mr. Chu, wanting to personally take him apart, but didn't see him anywhere.

The Krelp, ranging in sizes from baby whale to semi-trailer to jet plane, pressed closer to me. I hoped they had a plan. I hoped they could see me. I hoped they liked me as much as they liked Angel.

The dome cracked. The freezing ocean water rushed in in torrents, quickly filling one room after another. Just as someone activated the M-Geeks, readying them for battle, their quarters were flooded, water smashing them against the ceiling and sweeping them down hallways.

The section of dome over my mom's room started to split. I tensed, not really having a plan beyond "Get Mom, dead or alive." Water splashed in, dousing my mom's body. She moved.

She was alive!

The next moment, the ceiling above her broke open, and her room was instantly flooded. She got swept up against what was left of the ceiling, smashing against it hard. I heard her cry out with pain as I rushed in with the water, grabbing her shoulders and pulling her free. She was unconscious.

The Krelp hovered over us, and I realized they were creating a really big...snot bubble, sort of attached to several of them. Almost as if several kids were blowing bubbles, and the bubbles touched and poofed into a bigger, combined bubble. But with snot. Angel grabbed on to me, and before I had time to think, *Oh, man, I'm gonna barf,* the Krelp had dropped down beside the three of us. The bubble oozed around us, encasing us. There was air inside, and it kept the crushing ocean at bay.

Yes. I owed my life, Angel's life, and my mother's life to a mutant's ability to create industrial-strength snot.

The Krelp floated upward to where our sub was waiting, its air-lock doors open, and gently pushed us in. Immediately alarms sounded, the hatch doors started to close, and I felt pressurized air being pumped into the room.

Thirty seconds later, the air popped the bubble, the hatches were shut, and the inner doors swooshed open.

"Help my mom!" I cried to the medic who was already rushing in.

Fang ran in and knelt next to me, and then I was surrounded by the flock.

A few more seconds, and my mom started coughing and gagging, spitting salt water out. I patted her hand, praying that she would be all right. She looked thin, pale, weak, and beaten up, and a wildfire of rage swept through me as I thought of what they had put her through.

"Mom! It's me!" I said. "You're safe now. You're on a sub, and we're headed back to Hawaii." I couldn't believe we were together again at last, that she was alive, that we had reached her before it was too late.

Her brown eyes blinked groggily several times, and she winced as the medic started an IV in her arm. "Max?" she croaked.

"I'm right here," I said, holding her hand. My eyes felt hot, and I blinked several times.

Blearily, she looked up at me, tried to focus. "I knew . . . you'd come," she said.

My throat threatened to close, but I managed to say, "I'll always, always come, Mom. You can count on it."

My mom smiled faintly, then closed her eyes again.

Fang put his arm around me. "You did it. You saved her."

That was when I should have jumped up and done a victory dance, whooping my way down the corridor to the bathroom, where I could change into dry clothes.

Instead, I burst into unexpected tears, covering my eyes and gulping in breaths like a big baby. Fang put his arms around me.

Sometimes I just don't understand myself.

76

AS YOU MIGHT IMAGINE, I was *thrilled* to get off that submarine once and for all. We docked, the top hatch opened, and after the medics took my mom out on a stretcher, I was the next one off. I rushed up the ladder, over the gangplank to the dock, and then—

On the dock I wobbled, couldn't walk straight, and ended up falling over, feeling like I was going to hurl. I watched the medics hurrying away with my mom, and I would have to crawl to follow them.

Captain Perry knelt next to me. "You'll get your land legs back in no time," he said kindly.

Irony sort of reaches up and slaps you in the face sometimes, doesn't it?

Anyway, let's just resume our scene with me already sitting at a table, sucking down Fanta.

My mom was in the infirmary, where they had found she was way dehydrated, really banged up, and needed IV fluids and rest. Every time I realized she was back and alive, a new rush of warmth went through me.

And here I was with my flock, Fang's hand in mine beneath the table. Dejected because of his many failed attempts to create huge snot bubbles, Gazzy slumped in his seat. Nudge, Iggy, and Angel were on their fourth round of ice cream.

"Max!" Total raced up and jumped on a chair next to me. He enthusiastically licked my face, which, after being encased in a snot bubble, frankly didn't seem so bad. "Dude, I missed you guys so much! I'm so glad your mom is okay, Max. God knows the loss of a veterinarian would be a terrible thing. Ooh, Fanta!"

We got him his own Fanta and stuck a straw in it. He slurped it up delicately. "So much has happened," he said, wagging his short tail. "There's so much to tell you!"

I blinked. Total thought a lot had happened on *his* end? I felt like catching him up on *our* shenanigans would take about three weeks!

Akila ran up, leading John and Brigid to our table. She gave several short, happy barks, and Total turned to grin at me.

"Gotta go. Timmy's in the well. If you know what I mean." He winked and trotted off with Akila while we all tried very hard not to think too much about his last statement.

"Max! Max Max Max Max Max!!"

"Ella!" I got up and managed to run to my half sister without disgracing myself. We hugged each other, doing the weird rocking and patting motion that people do when they hug.

"Hello, Max."

I stopped rocking and patting. I would know that voice anywhere. I separated myself from Ella. "Jeb."

"Where's Mom?" Ella pleaded.

"Come on. I'll take you to her." Ignoring Jeb, I led Ella down the hallway toward the infirmary. I stopped outside her door, unable to resist looking through the glass to make sure she was still there and still all right. Ella and Jeb hurried in, and I hung back. Ella, at least, deserved some time alone with Mom. Already they were crying.

Smiling, feeling warm, dry, happy, and relatively safe, I headed back to the cafeteria. A dark, quick movement caught my eye, and I saw Brigid hurrying around a corner, her face tense.

I know spying on people is wrong and an invasion of their privacy, but fortunately I've never had a problem with that. I walked silently down the hall until I was close enough to the corner to peer around it at my nemesis.

Brigid was talking to some suits, gesturing earnestly with her hands. I pulled back. Suits always make me nervous.

I couldn't hear what they were saying, so I started to leave—but then someone else walked up to them and shook everyone's hands. Brigid greeted him, and the suits smiled and nodded.

It was Mr. Chu.

Beware of Mr. Chu, the Voice commanded like a foghorn booming inside my head. *And maybe Brigid.*

Maybe? I asked the Voice, incredulous. I would say, *definitely.*

Wouldn't you?

Epilogue

JUST LIKE HEAVEN

THE WIND SWEPT THROUGH my hair, and I closed my eyes, coasting on a thermal current, feeling the sun warming my face and my feathers.

Fang was above me, moving his wings in perfect unison with mine. We were holding hands: his was reaching down, and mine was reaching up.

Most of the flock was swimming in the ocean below us, in the shallow bay off the coast of Oahu. Some dolphins had joined them, no doubt lured by Angel. I could hear the flock's laughter, hear the cheerful chirping of the dolphins as they leaped out of the water.

"I'm glad Mom and Ella are home again safe. And I guess Jeb is—somewhere else." I didn't know whether Jeb was evil or not. He was totally confusing. Maybe I would never know.

"And I hear Total's off planning his and Akila's upcoming wedding," Fang added with a slight grin. "Guess what? You're maid of honor. Can't wait to see you in a poufy dress."

I ignored the jab. "Here's a more interesting piece of information: Brigid's at a news conference," I said. "I confronted her after I spotted her earlier. She said she was going to expose Mr. Chu."

"We'll see," said Fang, sounding somewhat disinterested, to my surprise and delight. "I guess we're finally alone"—a tiny smile curved his lips—"for the immediate future."

"Huh," I said, my heart kicking into high gear. "Huh. That's . . . nice."

Very, very carefully, Fang lowered himself even closer to me. I could almost feel his breath in my ear. We'd never flown this close to each other before. A delicate electric quiver ran down my spine.

Below us, a small golden head bobbed up and down in the water. I loved seeing Angel so happy, so carefree, not doing anything particularly evil at the moment.

"She really is special, isn't she?" I mused.

"Yes," he said. Fang switched hands, and I shook mine, trying to get some blood back into it.

"Maybe she really is the key to everything," I said, "whatever everything is. She keeps saying it's all about her. Maybe it really is."

"Max." Fang let go of my hand. "Right now, it's really all about—*us*."

He swooped down to the right in a big semicircle, ending facing me. Slowly we climbed upward, until we were almost vertical, flying straight up to the sun.

While carefully synchronizing our wings—they almost touched—Fang leaned in, gently put one hand behind my neck, and kissed me. It was just about as close to heaven as I'll ever get, I guess. I closed my eyes, lost in the feeling of flying and kissing and being with the one person in the world I completely, utterly trusted.

When we finally broke apart, we looked down at the others, who were way far below us now. Angel was shading her eyes, looking up at us with a big smile. She was sitting on a dolphin's back, and I hoped soon someone would explain to the dolphin that he shouldn't let Angel take advantage of his good nature.

Still looking up at us, Angel gave us a big thumbs-up.

"She approves," Fang said with a hint of amusement.

"Jeez," I wondered aloud. "Is that a good thing or a bad thing?"

Turn the page for a sneak preview of the hottest new James Patterson Pageturner series — a heart-stopping adventure featuring his most amazing characters yet…

Witch & Wizard

Coming December 2009

1

IT'S OVERWHELMING. A city's worth of angry faces staring at me like I'm a wicked criminal—which, I promise you, *I'm not*. The stadium is filled to capacity—*past* capacity. People are standing in the aisles, the stairwells, on the concrete ramparts, and a few extra thousand are camped out on the playing field. There are no football teams here today. They wouldn't be able to get out of the locker-room tunnels if they tried.

This total abomination is being broadcast on TV and on the Internet too. All the useless magazines are here, and the useless newspapers. Yep, I see cameramen in elevated roosts at intervals around the stadium.

There's even one of those remote-controlled cameras that runs around on wires above the field. There it is—hovering just in front of the stage, bobbing slightly in the breeze.

So, there are undoubtedly millions more eyes watching than I can see. But it's the ones here in the stadium that are breaking my heart. To be confronted with tens, maybe even hundreds of thousands of curious, uncaring, or at least indifferent, faces... talk about *frightening.*

And there are no moist eyes, never mind tears.

No words of protest.

No stomping feet.

No fists raised in solidarity.

No inkling that anybody's even thinking of surging forward, breaking through the security cordon, and carrying my family and me to safety.

Clearly, this is not a good day for us Allgoods.

In fact, as the countdown ticker flashes on the Jumbo-Tron displays at either end of the stadium, it's looking like this will be our *last* day.

It's a point driven home by the very tall, bald man up in the tower they've erected midfield—he looks like a cross between a Supreme Court chief justice and Ming the Merciless. I know who he is. I've actually met him. He's The One Who Is The One.

Directly behind his Oneness is a huge N.O. banner—*the New Order.*

And then the crowd begins to chant, almost sing, "The One Who Is The One! The One Who Is The One!"

Imperiously, The One raises his hand, and his hooded

lackeys on the stage push us forward, at least as far as the ropes around our necks will allow.

I see my brother, Whit, handsome and brave, looking down at the platform mechanism. Calculating if there's any way to jam it, some way to keep it from unlatching and dropping us to our neck-snapping deaths. Wondering if there's some last-minute way out of this.

I see my mother crying quietly. Not for herself, of course, but for Whit and me.

I see my father, his tall frame stooped with resignation, but smiling at me and my brother—trying to keep our spirits up, reminding us that there's no point in being miserable in our last moments on Earth.

But I'm getting ahead of myself. I'm supposed to be providing an *introduction* here, not the details of our public *execution.*

So let's go back a bit....